The Captive Knight

Lisa Ann Verge

Publishing History

First print edition published by Pocket Books as My Loving Enemy, © 1993
Second Print edition published by Bay Street Press LLC, © 2017 by Lisa Ann Verge
Print Edition formatted by Lisa Ann Verge
Cover design by Kim Killion

THE CAPTIVE KNIGHT

He Would Risk Everything For Her Love

After her dowry castle is seized as a prize of war, Aliénor's future is shattered. No dowry means no marriage, no escape from lifelong servitude, and no protection for her beloved, crippled brother.

But everything changes when her father captures a prisoner: The very same rogue knight who stole her lands...

About The Captive Knight

"A spirited heroine, a chivalric hero—exciting and passionate."
–Roberta Gellis, bestselling author of Masques of Gold

"Earthy, carnal tale. Electrifying reading."
–Rendezvous

***Don't miss Lisa Ann Verge's other passionate
historical romances!***

The Celtic Legends Series: Boxed Set
TWICE UPON A TIME: Book One
THE FAERY BRIDE: Book Two
WILD HIGHLAND MAGIC: Book Three
THE O'MADDEN: A Novella

Romantic Journeys Collection: Boxed Set
HEAVEN IN HIS ARMS
HER PIRATE HEART
SING ME HOME

The Cabin Fever Series
ALONE WITH YOU: Book One
LOST WITH YOU: Book Two
TAKEN WITH YOU: Book Three

Also available—the Novels of Lisa Verge Higgins

THE PROPER CARE AND MAINTENANCE OF
FRIENDSHIP
ONE GOOD FRIEND DESERVES ANOTHER
FRIENDSHIP MAKES THE HEART GROW
FONDER
RANDOM ACTS OF KINDNESS
SENSELESS ACTS OF BEAUTY

CHAPTER ONE

Gascony, 1355

"It's him, my lady," shouted a knight from the ramparts of the castle. "Your father is coming home!"

Squinting up from the courtyard below, Aliénor de Tournan paused from marking the symbol of her father's house on a barrel of grapes. Her fingers tightened on the chalk as her heart clenched. She'd been waiting for her father for weeks, and every day's delay had filled her with anxiety. But now that he'd been spotted, she shuddered under a new and different kind of fear.

Waving acknowledgement to the knight, she shoved the chalk in her pocket and strode across the courtyard. As the only daughter of a motherless house, she would be expected to present a grand dinner, have a new wine barrel tapped, and arrange pallets in the main hall for the returning warriors.

But her wayward feet weren't leading her to the center tower of the castle, where her true duty lay. No, they were leading her to the shadow of the stables, her beloved palfrey, and a recklessness that she would surely pay for later.

Fumbling with the saddle, she tossed it across the back of her horse, hurrying to buckle it before the stable master saw what she was doing. Mounting, Aliénor urged the mare into the courtyard and then gave the beast a nudge before any good-hearted soul could shout for her to come back. A page scurried out of the way as the horse's hooves clattered on the wooden drawbridge.

Tearing across the open field before the castle, high on a cliff, she let the wind blow through her hair as she gazed over the rolling lands of her family's domain. To the west lay the silver ribbon of the river Arrats, which curved its way around the castle hill. To the south she could see the faintest outline of the Pyrenees in the crystalline air. And the long, fertile valley between gleamed a pale ochre, the harvest down to stubble.

She nudged her horse down the cliff side path where fig trees blocked the view. Only when she reached the bottom of the hill and approached the village did she see the first bobbing spike of a blue and green banner between the half-timbered houses.

Father!

The mare must have felt her jittery excitement,

for the horse lurched toward the village with new vigor. Aliénor strained her neck trying to count the number of mounted men, but the winding streets thwarted her. It wasn't as if the total would give any hint if her father had been victorious, or whether her future offered a fresh bridal wreath or the cold shroud of a convent veil. God's Blood, she was acting as superstitious as the kitchen maids, trying to pick out the profiles of their future husbands in the hearth ashes.

Her father emerged from around the last bend and her heart fluttered like a startled bird. Though there was no blood on his tunic, the fabric of his sleeve was torn and there was a new dent in his helmet. There had been a struggle, a fight, perhaps even a battle.

"Father," she blurted, as she rode up to shorten the space between them. "Did you capture my dowry castle?"

The Viscount of Tournan took his time unhooking the chain-mail curtain attached to his helmet before lifting the bascinet off his head. A scarlet slash marred his cheek and nose, discoloring his swarthy, hard-planed face. He handed his helmet back to his squire as he fixed his black gaze upon her.

"So this is how you greet me, daughter."

She swallowed, sensing the darkness of his mood. "Forgive me, Father, but—"

"I should think those nuns would have taught you better in your youth." His gaze flickered to her empty hands. "You didn't even think to bring me wine."

He spurred his charger and shot past her. She breathed hard, trying to squeeze her spirit into the restraints her father demanded. Provoking him was dangerous, even for her. But she had spent the years since her father had returned wounded from the battle of Crécy studying his fluxing moods, his hot temper, and his tendency to rage. She knew his limits down to the last breaking straw.

So she turned her mare around and came up beside him. "I beg your indulgence, father. Patience is not one of my virtues—"

"We've ridden hard this day, and fought harder, all for your sake."

"I'm very grateful—"

"We did *not* capture the castle."

A painful buzzing started in her head.

"Castétis was strongly guarded." Her father's unshaven jaw tightened. "It was impossible to assault, impossible to seize, impossible to recapture without a significantly larger force than I had with me."

She gripped the pommel and watched her knuckles whiten.

"Nonetheless," he continued, "men have been wounded, Aliénor. Men have died—all for your sake."

God's Blood, no. She twisted on the saddle, searching the line of men behind her for beloved, missing faces while her vision went blurry.

"Do you believe I failed you, girl?"

"You did not fail me, father." But her heart was not in the words but in her mouth as she counted helmeted heads.

"Indeed, I did not fail you. Are you listening to me?"

She turned back to him. "I'm listening, father." Not a man missing, it seemed, but the road was so narrow she couldn't be sure.

He said, "I captured something better than the castle."

She started.

"I captured the thief who stole it in the first place—that lowborn, sell-sword bastard of a usurper."

On a gasp, she said, "The English knight?"

"Indeed." Her father's smile was a slash of ill-humor. "Jehan de St. Simon is in my custody. I will ransom the knight for Castétis, and then you, my unruly, impatient, doubting daughter, you will have your dowry castle once again."

He kicked his charger up the steepest and narrowest part of the slope, dismissing her. She fell into place behind him as the implications of his news sank in. Could it be true that she wouldn't be ushered off to a convent? Could it be true that she wouldn't forever be a servant in her father's house? That she would have a home of her own, where she and her brother Laurent could live in peace, safety, and maybe with even a glimmer of happiness?

A slow excitement filled her. Reaching the top of

the hillock, she thundered across the field in her father's wake, not stopping until she reached the courtyard. She dismounted in a sliding rush, tossing the reins to a stable boy. All but dancing to the steps of the donjon—the main tower—she joined her frowning father as they watched the other knights file in. She couldn't *wait* to lay eyes upon the English thief. She had a mouthful of accusations for the man who'd stolen her future one year ago, and not a single one of them was maidenly.

The thief, slumped on his tethered horse, was the last to come into view. He wore a short tunic over his chain mail but the cloth was so dirty she couldn't see the colors of his heraldry. As he was led closer to where she and her father stood, she noticed the dirt was reddish-brown.

The angry words she'd summoned stuck in her throat, followed by a deepening concern. The prisoner was barely conscious.

"He dared to battle us all," her father bellowed to the gathered men and servants. "No man can steal from me without punishment, eh, St. Simon?"

The prisoner didn't move. Fresh blood dripped in a rivulet over the steel of his shoes. A short, sharp quiver of fear speared through her. If the knight was still bleeding, he might very well die.

"Away from him, girl. *Now.*"

Halfway down the stairs she stopped short, her blood running cold. She was all too familiar with the tone of voice coming out of her father's mouth.

"Tend my wounded," he barked, "not my enemy."

"But father—"

"I'll rain hell on any man—or woman—who aids him."

Her father swept up the stairs, his metal shoes clanking on the weathered stones. She remained where she was until the heavy oak door of the donjon closed behind him. Only then did she turn to his men-at-arms, questioning silently. To the last, they averted their gazes, busying themselves by pulling the wounded thief off the horse and carrying him, limp and dripping a trail of blood, toward the cells of the northwest tower.

Something terrible had happened at Castétis. Something done, no doubt, in a white-blind rage so fierce that her father had forgotten one vital point: A dead prisoner couldn't pay ransom.

Jehan de St. Simon was her worst enemy.

Yet she had to make sure he lived.

***

Aliénor waited late into the night for the muted sounds of drunkenness to die in the great hall. When the last voice had faded into silence, she tossed off the fur coverlet and pulled open the velvet curtains surrounding her bed. Her chamber lay at the rear of the castle, lit by two arrow-slits along with the dim glow of burning embers in the hearth. Margot, her chambermaid, slept soundly on her pallet.

Aliénor shoved her feet into slippers and seized the sack she'd hidden under her pillow. Picking up an unlit tallow candle, she slipped over the dry rushes and unhooked her fur-lined mantle from the peg by the door. The rush lights in the hall had sputtered out hours before, but she knew the stairs well and had no need of light to make her way. At the bottom, she paused to slip on her mantle while listening for sounds in the pantry or the buttery. When she was sure all was still, she headed through the narrow passage, past the screens, into the great hall.

The embers of a fire still glowed in the massive fireplace, throwing a red-orange light over her father's sleeping men-at-arms. One of the mastiffs lifted his head and sniffed the air as she crossed the hall. As she reached the arched wooden door, she heard the click of hounds' nails as, one by one, more dogs rose from their slumber. Unable to order them to stay without alerting the sleeping knights, she pushed open the door and herded them out into the chill October air and then closed the door behind her.

The courtyard was bathed in bluish starlight. The frigid wind from the Pyrenees—the *autan* wind— swept through, scattering dried leaves. *Bent d'autan, ploujo douman,* she thought, absently repeating the peasant prediction of rain. Shivering, she descended the stairs to the courtyard and headed toward the warmth of the kitchens.

Inside on the work tables, wrapped in linen, were

the remnants of the evening's feast: chicken and pork pies, large, half-eaten chunks of boiled beef, rectangular loaves of trencher bread, and earthen jugs of hippocras, the heady spiced wine her father liked too much. The dogs lifted their noses and trotted to the tables, but with a hiss from her they hung back. Fortunately, the servants were accustomed to people entering and leaving the room to indulge late-night appetites, and they slept through any interruption. Aliénor peered through the sleeping servants until she found one large figure lying apart from the others. She bent close to him.

"Hugo," she whispered, touching his shoulder. "Wake up, Hugo."

The boy's eyes opened, then widened as they focused.

She lifted a finger to his lips so he wouldn't make a sound. "I need your help."

Hugo nodded, still groggy with sleep. As he rose from his makeshift bed of dried hay she was once again struck by how much he'd grown. Hugo's mind was like a child's, but his body was no longer so. Years ago, she'd rescued Hugo from the brutal, teasing wrath of the village boys and brought him into the castle service. If those boys could see him now, they wouldn't dare tie the brawny orphan to a Maypole and singe him with glowing ends of tinder.

She handed Hugo a wooden platter and pointed to what she wanted. The boy loaded a large piece of cold meat, a loaf of trencher bread, the ashen carcass of a well-cooked duck, and a jug of hippocras and another of water onto the tray. She dipped the wick of her tallow candle into the embers in one of the fireplaces and then, with her dogs and Hugo in tow, she left the warm kitchen.

The dogs jumped and whined, the scent of food in their nostrils. Aliénor clicked her tongue until they were silenced and then shredded some of the duck to distract them while she and Hugo slipped away and passed through the door of the northwest tower. Once inside, she saw a faint glow at the bottom of the spiral staircase.

She shielded her candle from eddies of wind and descended, the nape of her neck prickling. It was here where she and her mother had housed and tended many victims of the plague during the last wave of sickness, back when they thought it would help to keep the suffering away from the healthy. But the villagers had fallen like sheaves of wheat both here and in the fields, and her two older brothers had died from the plague in these rooms. Though the last of the victims had died six years before, imprinted in the air was a miasma of suffering.

A ghostly voice floated up the stairs, startling her. "Who goes there?"

"The daughter of the house," she said, bracing herself. "I've brought food for the prisoner."

She rounded the last curve to face the guard at the doorway of the cell. His sword was sheathed, but his hand lay on the hilt.

He released his weapon as he saw her. "My lord ordered that no one is to see the prisoner."

"But certainly he needs to eat, Sir Rudel."

The guard swayed a bit, as if he had drunk too much wine from the freshly tapped cask at dinner. "My lord ordered—"

"My father is not himself today," she interrupted. "Surely you understand? In the excitement of victory, he neglected common courtesy—"

"He told me not to feed him."

She feigned surprise, though she too had heard her father's angry orders. Most of the castle had, since he'd roared them across the trestle tables when one of his vassals, Sir Rostand, had requested permission to tend to the prisoner's welfare. Behind the screens where she had tended the wounded men, Aliénor couldn't coax any of them into divulging what had happened at Castétis, but their censure and disapproval of her father was palpable.

"Rudel," she said, "you've been my father's vassal for many years. Surely you recognize this rage will pass, like every other."

"So will my life, if I defy his orders."

"Do you prefer to be punished by my father's hand or to die by the sword of the Prince of Wales?"

The guard quieted. Her father was a staunch supporter of the French king, but the wounded thief was a vassal of the English Prince of Wales. She thought it highly unlikely that a mighty prince, heir to the English throne, would turn his face away from more weighty matters to concern himself in the fate of a single knight in the wilds of Gascony. But considering her father's rage, she figured she needed all the leverage she could get to convince Rudel to grant her access.

She leaned in and placed her free hand on his arm. "No need to tell my father I was here, of course," she said. "Best for both of us, I think."

"But if St. Simon harms you—"

"The knight is hardly in any condition to attack. Besides, Hugo is here."

She gestured into the gloom behind her. The guard looked at the looming boy-man and his laden tray.

"And from what little I saw," she added, pressing her advantage, "the knight may already be dead."

The guard frowned. With some reluctance, he pulled out the iron key hanging around his neck. He fumbled with it until it scraped into the lock. Yanking the door wide, he took the tallow candle from Aliénor's hand, thrust it into the small room, and glanced about as he gripped his sword.

She saw a body lying motionless against the far wall. Approaching the knight, she sank to her knees an arm's length away. He was a large man, broader of shoulder and longer of limb than she had noticed when he'd been slumped on his horse in the courtyard. He still wore his chain mail and armor plates at his elbows and knees, but his baldric and all its attached weapons had been removed. Congealed blood covered his features.

She reached out to touch his face, biting her lip in fear it would be cold and lifeless under her hand.

He moved so fast she barely became aware of the motion until her fingers flared out at the pain of his grip.

"Call off your guards, woman, or I shall shatter every bone in your wrist."

CHAPTER TWO

"*U*nhand me."

Aliénor spoke firmly even as her hand went numb. His eyes, fogged with pain, bored into hers from beneath his matted hair. Terror made her insides soft, but for eight years she'd run a castle full of fighting men under the capricious rule of her mercurial father. She knew better than to show fear.

Suddenly the room rang with the sound of a sword being scraped out of a scabbard.

"Don't." She threw up her free hand to stop Rudel from approaching. "The prisoner will come to his senses."

That cloudy blue gaze flickered to the men looming behind her. Rudel shuffled uneasily under her restraint. Hugo made low grunting noises. Then those eyes shifted back to look her over from scalp to knees.

"What's this mischief?" he rasped. "Does the viscount send a woman to kill me?"

"I am unarmed." She twisted her torso so he could see she wore no dagger. Then she tipped her head to where Hugo had placed the tray. "I have brought food and wine and the means to tend to your wounds."

"Not by his orders," he retorted. "That murderer would sooner send his maiden daughter to share my bed."

A flush blistered her cheeks. The gall of the man to speak so, even if he didn't know who she was. "It's the viscount's food," she insisted, "the viscount's wine—"

"—sent by another knight. One of the viscount's better men. Sir Rostand, perhaps," he said, "or another?"

"Does it matter, if it fills your belly?" The tips of her fingers began to tingle.

"I trust no gift from Tournan." His gaze dipped to the gape of her surcoat with a speculative gleam. "Unless he's seeking forgiveness by offering you up–"

"Accept my hospitality—or don't," she interrupted. "But release me now, or my guard will relieve you of your hand."

His jaw hardened and he breathed hard, like the huff of a buck. With a grunt, he loosed his grip. She tumbled onto one hip. Righting herself, she gestured for Hugo to bring the wine.

Rubbing the blood back into her wrist, she

watched as Sir Jehan pushed himself up to a sitting position, wincing all the way. He took the jug Hugo offered to him and lifted it by the handle. His hand shook, making droplets run over his chin and spill upon his chest.

Mad with pain, she thought, her heart still pounding. Mad with thirst. And she was the maddest of all, to have expected calm, reason, or gratitude.

She slid out of his reach to remove his metal shoes, gathering her wits while she mentally listed his wounds. Blood soaked through his chain-mail hose where broken links revealed a cut on his thigh. His left hand lay bruised and swollen by his side. She wondered if the bones were broken or crushed, but she was more concerned with the wound still seeping on his head and, more alarming, the source of all the blood soaking his surcoat.

How could he have been wounded so seriously on the torso? Swords were nearly useless against mail, and if this knight wore a coat-of-plates, as most knights did, the daggers that might break chain mail at close contact could not possibly have penetrated the plate defenses.

She would find out soon enough, she thought, as she removed his round knee-plates. He breathed hard as he sagged against the wall, alert in the way of a man trying to battle unconsciousness. She ordered Hugo to bring the platter of food closer to give the thief something else to do than stare.

"No poison here?" he said, tearing into a duck's

leg.

"Poison's a coward's weapon."

"A woman's one, too."

She flung his knee-plates away so they clattered on the stone floor.

"No poisoned wine, no poisoned food, and no dagger in my heart," he said. "It's a daring woman who'll defy the Viscount of Tournan."

She frowned, annoyed he knew her father's nature so well. "Lean forward so I can remove your surcoat."

He canted away from the wall. Pain spasmed across his face. He raised his arms, favoring his swollen hand, so she could lift the bloody rag over his head. He wore no coat-of-plates beneath the tunic, which was odd, and the links in his chain mail were broken in a few places. That meant the wounds on his abdomen must be from daggers.

For his sake, she hoped they were not deep.

"The viscount caught us when we were riding down a roebuck," he said. "Neither I nor my men were fully armored."

She ignored the fact that he'd read her mind and reached for the buckles on his shirt of mail.

He placed his rough, swollen hand over hers. "It will not be a pleasant sight for such pretty eyes."

"I've surely seen worse wounds on my father."

A half-smile cracked the dried blood upon his cheek. "I knew you for a knight's daughter."

She pulled her hand from under his. "Your

behavior suggested otherwise."

"Perhaps I'm not at my best."

She wondered when a thief would be at his best. When stealing unguarded castles? Destroying a woman's future?

"Since it appears your motives are honest," he said, in a low voice, "let's begin again. Tell me your name, mademoiselle."

"It hardly matters."

"It matters to me. I would know who I should thank."

"Very well." She couldn't help herself. "My name is Aliénor. Aliénor de Tournan."

He stilled, his half-smile fading. It felt good to throw her name at him, as foolish as it was. Cursing the man to his face felt better than cursing his name, even if it did thin the air in the room and make his gaze turn to blue flames.

He rasped, "Leave."

"You reject my hospitality?"

"Tournan and hospitality are two words that don't belong together."

"I am chatelaine of this castle," she said, falling back on her heels, "and I will do as my mother taught me: Care for all who come to our gates. Even thieves."

He loomed forward, close enough for her to see the bristles of his dark beard beneath the blood and dirt streaking his face, close enough to see his dilated pupils, and the stark pain in his eyes.

"Easy, Hugo," she said, as the boy's grunting noises heightened in pitch. "Sir Jehan can do me no harm."

The thief's gaze flickered brighter. "You have more courage than your father."

"You are as weak as a newborn colt."

"Even a newborn colt can crush a flower."

"Are you going to parry words with me, thief, or are you going to allow me to bind your wounds?"

"Only a fool would trust a Tournan."

"I have good reason to see you live." Her voice hardened. "Castétis is my dowry. Only if you live can we ransom you for my stolen castle."

She refused to lower her gaze though her heart pounded in her ears. The knight had long, dark lashes and strong, straight brows. His eyes had a lazy tilt at the corners that spoke of a nature far more sensual than the one he radiated right now. On the side where his head wound hadn't bled all over his face, she saw shallow, pale creases fanning from the corner of his eye, a hint of mirth and good humor her mind balked at imagining.

"I will test your skill first," he said, sinking against the wall. "Start with my head wound."

She rose to her feet to fetch what she needed, hating how her knees wobbled. She'd seen knights in this pain-crazed condition before. It was a wonder he could muster any strength at all. But the threat of his unpredictable strength, combined with her anger at him, her shock at his condition, and a growing dread that she might not be able to save his life conspired to unsettle her both in mind and body.

She took her time collecting a pitcher of water and a stack of linens before returning to kneel beside him. She searched through his matted locks for the slash that had bled so profusely. She found it at the edge of his forehead, spreading from just above his brow to the tip of his right ear. As she removed the mask of dirt and blood, it became clear he was a young knight, not many years older than she. She had always imagined this wretched thief as older, gnarled, and war-scarred, with a body as weak as his honor.

"Hugo," she murmured, "go to the kitchens and fetch more wine." When she heard no motion behind her, she twisted and raised a brow at the boy, who was shaking his head. "Rudel will watch over me while you are away."

Hugo shook his head harder, his dark hair swinging around his face.

"Do as she bids, good man," the thief said. "On my honor, I will not harm your mistress."

Acid bit the back of her throat at the talk of honor from a thief, but his steady words had a different effect on Hugo. The boy paused for a moment, then took the earthen pitcher at her side and silently left the room.

She shook her head.

Men.

She threaded her silver needle in preparation for stitching his head wound. He twitched at the first piercing. Fresh blood dripped and she knew from the tautness of his body she was causing him pain. She shouldn't care. For the trouble he'd caused her, she should enjoy every bit of agony she inflicted on him. Yet she found herself working swiftly, finishing just as Hugo returned with more wine.

"It's done," she said, as she secured a clean linen strip around his head. "Now let me see your hand."

Grudgingly, he presented it to her. She probed the swelling around his wrist. She felt no broken bones but suspected his wrist was sprained. There wasn't much she could do but wrap it up.

When she was done, she gave his chain-mail shirt a tug. "Do you still fear I'll plunge a dagger into your heart?"

He waved his good hand. She couldn't help but notice it was shaking. Alarmed, she made short work with the buckles and then, with Hugo's help, she pulled the chain mail off his shoulders. A padded doublet followed. While she dragged the heavy chain mail and the doublet to the pile with his other armor, Hugo helped wrestle the knight out of his bloody shift. When she turned around, Sir Jehan was naked from the waist up.

Her throat went dry. The knight didn't need padding and plates for protection. Surely any sword would deflect off the iron-hard sweep of his shoulders and the sculptured planes and ripples of his torso. Her gaze fell to his abdomen, tacky with dried blood, and the odd thoughts fled.

"Tell me, daughter of Tournan," he said. "Does *this* look like the result of a fair fight between knights?"

She held her tongue, for the pallor of his face and the quaver in his voice suggested she was running out of time. Dropping to her knees beside him again, she swiped a wet linen over the swollen ripples of his abdomen to expose the skin beneath, searching for open bleeding, preparing to stanch it. But beneath her hand, the sheen of dried blood gave way to nothing but an abdomen discolored with bruises. For all her efforts, she couldn't find any wound deeper than a scratch.

She paused, baffled, the wet linen dripping in her hand. A blow of a spiked mace atop chain mail could cause bruising, or a blow of a mailed fist, but that didn't explain the source of the blood in which he and his clothes were covered.

"No words from the loyal daughter?" He was breathing fast, staring at her like she was his only grip on consciousness.

"I'll tend to your leg and be on my way." She tossed the linen aside and reached for her needle. "I'll leave the food. I don't know when I can return."

"Not a single question? No curiosity as to whose blood I'm bathed in?"

She wanted to ask. She wasn't sure she wanted to know.

"Ask your father," the thief persisted. "Ask him why he battled a knight who'd offered up his sword."

"Enough."

"Ask him," he persisted, "why he butchered three of my men before my eyes, as well as an innocent, unarmed squire."

***

The next morning, Aliénor caught up with her brother, sprawled on the bottom stair of the castle steps. After last night's troubling confession from Sir Jehan—one that kept her awake most of the night—Aliénor was determined to turn her mind to the more solvable problem of the fifteen-year-old Laurent de Tournan.

She sank onto the stairs beside him. "Father is still off hunting then?"

"He left before dawn," her brother said, shrugging. "He still hasn't asked to see me."

"Good."

Her father's inattention was a small reprieve, but it would not last for long. Sometime today she was sure he would summon his only remaining male heir into his presence, and then Laurent would face the usual reckoning.

She glanced at Laurent's saddled horse standing nearby. "I see Thibaud has arranged for practice."

"Always the optimist, our uncle." With a wry smile, he turned over in his hand a small block of oak on which he was carving the face of a saint. "He thinks that playing at knights' games will turn me from my intentions."

She gave him a narrow look. "Thibaud thinks training you as a knight will keep our father in better humor."

"A fool's errand."

"Don't poke the beast, Laurent, not today." She dipped down, forcing her brother to meet her eyes. "On the madness scale, our father is well past St. Stephen's Day and nearly at Epiphany."

"Skipping straight past Christmas?"

"Alas."

"But he's not as furious as Good Friday, you think?"

She pulled a face, thinking of the many gradations of her father's madness, measured by her and Laurent's own private scale. "If the condition of the knight in the tower is any measure, we should both be on our best behavior at all times."

"In that case, I'll put off reminding our father of his promise to send me to a monastery."

His words did nothing to assuage her unease. Father had made the promise to Laurent as a child, long ago, when things were different. Before the plague had taken their two older brothers and made Laurent the heir.

"Oh, don't brood, Aliénor," he said, his voice light. "I will hold onto hope still, no matter what you think. After all, father hasn't sent me off to any local lord as squire. I'm nearly fifteen and still living in his house. Certainly that means—"

"—nothing more than father—when not fighting for King Jean—spends too much time offering up his sword to foreign lords rather than seeing to his responsibilities here." She tried to brush his hair out of his face but Laurent veered away from her touch with a scowl. "Now that he's back," she said, "it's just as likely he'll secure your future at someone's court. Maybe even the Count of Armagnac."

"The count may not be pleased to have such a squire." He gathered up the length of his woolen tunic, the one that looked very much like a monk's robe, to expose his twisted foot, which tugged the soft leather of his boot into strange angles. "Have you ever known a crippled knight?"

"Your leg is only a problem when you're fighting on the ground," she said. "You know very well, on a horse, there is no difference. Knights fight on horseback, not on foot."

"Unless they're unseated."

"Which you will rarely be," she added, nodding toward the waiting horse, "if you practice in the saddle."

"But I'm not Bertrand." He placed the block of wood aside. "And I'm not Gaston. Do you remember how they rode, Aliénor? How easy upon the saddle, how swift across the fields?"

For a moment she could almost see them, her two husky, dark-haired older brothers, racing one another through the gates of the castle, the shod hooves of their mounts ringing upon the flagstones.

"It's no secret," he said, into their shared memory, "that father wishes the plague had taken me instead of them."

"Don't say such things." The words came out by rote for the many times she'd denied their terrible truth. "It will make you bitter, Laurent. Hard-hearted. It will twist you up inside until you're no better than…"

Our father.

"You're right, of course. I should say penance." He squinted up at her from under a fringe of dark hair and flashed a grin like a splinter in her heart. "I'd rather go to the chapel and say penance than practice."

His ploy was so plain that she couldn't help but return his smile. "Practice first, penance later."

"You're a worse taskmaster than Thibaud."

"Thibaud would have you on the horse already instead of sitting here wasting time wondering about our fate."

"Ally, I may wonder about my fate, but you have no reason to do so anymore. Father will find you a husband as soon as he ransoms the prisoner for your castle."

She resisted the urge to wince. She had no reason to feel guilty. She was not the one who'd murdered an unarmed squire, but blood-guilt couldn't help but tarnish all her pretty expectations.

"If father plans to marry me off, he'd best do it quickly." She gestured to the courtyard, cluttered around the perimeter with the village *rentes*: bags of grain, huge bundles of wood from the forests on the northern slopes, oak barrels of new wine, and sundry foodstuffs she was long overdue to sort and store. Amid the piles were barrels of pitch and sheaves of arrows. "By the looks of things, he's expecting to hold off an attack."

Laurent's black eyes, so like his father's, rounded. "Do you think the Prince of Wales will march his army here?"

"If he does, we'll be well prepared."

The words tripped off her tongue but her mind traveled a darker path. It had been over a century since this castle had seen battle, if Thibaud's histories were to be trusted. Now she wondered about the line of trees close outside the northwest wall, thick enough for archers to hide behind. The mortar had been crumbling amid the crenellations of the southwest tower for years, but father had not been here to order restoration. And the drawbridge spanned hard-packed earth instead of the deep ditch that had once been there, if Thibaud's stories were true.

Then booming laughter rang out in the courtyard, distracting her from growing worries. Their uncle strode into sight from around the shadow of the donjon. Thibaud always reminded Aliénor of a badly wound spool of white woolen thread. His head, with its great mane of stark white hair, was disproportionally larger than his body, which appeared as lean and hard as a young man's. Despite his sixty years of age, her late mother's uncle was anything but weak. His penetrating gray eyes saw as sharply as a man half his age, and despite occasional bouts of stiffness, he was as adroit on a stallion as any newly dubbed knight.

"There you are, uncle." She tilted her head toward Laurent, now sighing and shaking his head. "Help me persuade my stubborn little brother that even monks need to know how to ride well."

"True monks travel the world on foot," Laurent said, squinting up at his kinsman, "and they never ride horses."

"Listen to you, talking about traveling the world on foot." The older man reached down and gave Laurent's twisted limb a good pull. "Are you to walk from here to Toulouse on such a leg? A good monk would ride well, to better help the poor in all places."

"You know I can ride circles around you, uncle—"

"But not with a lance."

"A lance is a knight's weapon."

"Have you noticed there's been a war on for the last thirty years? That the English king still won't pay homage to our own good King Jean? That the damn English king has sent his spawn, the Prince of Wales, to punish those who pay homage to our own true king? That women, children, peasants, and even monks with crippled legs won't be spared?"

Her brother sighed. "History lessons are after

nones, uncle."

"Any man who travels, either to make war or to pray for the souls of men, must protect himself."

"My prayers shall protect me."

"So shall a lance."

"Come now, uncle, a lance is a tournament toy–"

"Perhaps it is, perhaps it isn't. Now climb on your horse or I'll toss you on it myself."

Laurent rolled his eyes but dutifully pushed himself up from the stairs, stowing his knife and carving in a pocket. Limping over to the horse, he climbed onto a half-cask and waved away a stable boy's offer of aid. With practiced awkwardness, he swung his twisted leg over the horse and sat in the saddle.

"Warm him up with a few circuits," Thibaud said. "Get him firm under your seat."

Laurent kicked the horse and set him on his paces. Aliénor stood up from her seat on the stairs and took a place next to Thibaud.

Her uncle leaned closer. "I trust you know what you're doing, woman?"

"Laurent can't hide in the chapel forever. Father will summon him eventually. Best to choose the time and situation."

"Later is usually better. Like when your father is out of his cups."

"Such as in the morning," she said pointedly, "after a hunt. He's always happy after a hunt, whether he fells a deer or not. And this way, my father will see

Laurent on horseback, rather than glimpsing him limping across the yard or at prayer in the chapel."

Thibaud grunted.

"And where have you been hiding, uncle? I've been trying to talk to you since dawn."

"I have more important things to do than teach your brother how to ride a horse in circles." He gave her a sidelong look. "I wouldn't have come here at all if I didn't see the boy was getting the best of you."

She raised her brows. "That's a poor excuse for trying to avoid me."

"So you couldn't charm or cajole the men-at-arms into telling you anything, eh?"

"You'd think I was carrying the plague, by how quickly they turned away when I approached."

"You're his daughter. They know they'll lose more than their tongues if they utter a word."

Thibaud went silent, by all appearances focused on watching Laurent put the horse through his paces. The ends of Thibaud's unfashionably long surcoat flapped in the breeze blowing over the toothed edge of the ramparts. In the bright sunlight, she could see every crease in his well-lined face. She waited, knowing if she remained patient for long enough, her voluble uncle wouldn't be able to bear the silence.

"What I know I heard in pieces." His bushy brows, as white as summer clouds, lowered over his eyes. "Your father trapped Sir Jehan and his men in a valley near the Garonne River. Sir Jehan and his men were lightly armed and not expecting an ambush. The

knight had no choice but to surrender, and he did."
Thibaud's cheek flexed under a prickly field of white
stubble. "Then your father set his mercenaries upon
them all."

"Mercenaries?!"

"Picked up along the way, so Sir Rostand told
me. A rough, bloody group of sell-swords. Your
father wanted to present a larger force at the gates of
Castétis, so he hired a dozen or so upon the road."

Father had said something about men having
died for her sake, but every knight of the household
had returned. Her father must have meant some of
those mercenaries, hungry creatures, men-at-arms set
adrift from their liege lord between campaigns.

"At your father's orders," Thibaud continued,
"they killed Sir Jehan's men."

A pinch brought her attention to her hands and
she realized she was digging her nails into her palms.
"Surely father must have been provoked—"

"A flea could provoke him," Thibaud said. "Or
too much spice in the wine. Or a thwarted conquest, a
drunken insult, a sidelong glance—"

"Thibaud."

She could not defend her father's behavior, but it
still felt like treason to enumerate his mistakes. She
still remembered a time when her father wasn't like
this, before Crécy, when he was kind and patient and
full of laughter.

"Sir Jehan fought," her uncle continued, "as any
man would. His squire ran in to defend his master

with no more weapons than his fists. The mercenaries made short work of the boy."

She winced. In her heart, she had known Sir Jehan's words were true, but she'd hoped for some excuse, some twist, some less horrific version of the truth.

She said, "I don't"—*want to*—"believe that."

"Yes, you do." He hefted a lance to get Laurent's attention. "You've seen the knight, bathed in the blood of his own men. You've seen him, beaten senseless. As surely as I saw you wander to the northwest tower last night."

Thibaud's gray eyes bored into her, and though she tried to still her expression, she knew she'd given herself away.

"Old bones don't sleep well, especially when the winter is nigh." He held out the lance, hilt first, as Laurent swung by on a circuit and paused long enough to grasp it. Her brother tucked the lance under his arm, adjusted to the weight of it, and kicked the horse into a trot again before Thibaud continued. "You've been known to nurture a half-dead dog back to life, so I knew you wouldn't allow a knight to die of battle wounds."

"You think too well of me. If Sir Jehan had died, I'd be further away from my dowry and closer to a convent."

"And it's an earthly husband you want, is it?"

"Where's the sin in that?" She wouldn't blush, she *wouldn't*. "I would have a castle of my own, and for that I need my equal as a husband. I would have a roof over my head, perhaps children, and the kind of happiness that once rang within these walls. Do you remember those days, Thibaud?"

She remembered them. She held them close like a light in the darkness. During Easter and Christmas in those before-days, she used to be released from the convent, her brother Bertrand from his service as squire, and they'd all come home for the season. Bertrand would strut about in his fine silk doublet, joking with the men-at-arms. Gaston would swing Laurent up on his shoulders to give him pony rides around the courtyard. Her mother sat by the fire after every meal, her golden head bent over her embroidery. And her father would reveal gifts brought from far-away places, pieces of armor from Venetian metal workers, fur mantles from Normandy, a specially-made etched leather saddle for Laurent's first pony.

Then the battle at Crécy happened, and father returned months later with a dent in his skull and rages that could not be controlled.

"Castétis is not much," she said, "but it could be a refuge. For me. For Laurent. And for you, uncle, if it suits you. We would all have a life away from my father's… capricious nature."

"And what makes you think your father will let you go?"

She opened her mouth to ask what he meant, but Thibaud's attention had turned to the portal. She heard the baying of hounds and the clatter of hooves over the drawbridge just before her father galloped into the courtyard with his hunting dogs at heel. Her father's gaze swept the courtyard with masterly pride, and then stilled on Laurent.

Her heart crowded into her throat as her father kicked his mount between Laurent and a bale of hay, hemming him in.

"So my son has emerged from hiding." He glanced around the courtyard, taking in the target raised on the opposite side. "And here you are, training to be a knight."

She curled her hands within the folds of her kirtle, willing her brother to be wise. From this distance, she could see the pallor of Laurent's face.

"By all means, continue." Her father dismounted and tossed the reins to a stable boy, then tugged the riding glove from his hand, finger by finger. "Show me what you've learned while I was away fighting for your legacy."

Her breath came shallow between her lips. It would have been better if her father had returned from the hunt while Laurent was in swordplay with Thibaud. Laurent looked lively and impressive while parrying from the saddle, but he was good enough with the lance. That's what she told herself, over and over, as Laurent nudged his gelding to the head of the cleared area. His black eyes shone with what looked encouragingly like determination.

"Hold the lance tight," Thibaud shouted. "Raise

the tip as you aim for the center of the target."

Laurent's horse pranced while her brother tried to settle him.

Come, frai. *Show him what you can do. You're long due to be sent off to squire, someplace far from here, where he can't hurt you anymore.*

Laurent dug his heels into the horse's sides. The gelding broke into a canter, kicking up puffs of dust. Laurent held up the lance as Thibaud instructed, though the tip quivered as if he struggled with the weight. She watched with bated breath as the point of the lance tore into the edge of the woven bag and grain spilled out onto the ground.

For the space of a heartbeat, she thought, *he has hit the target well,* but then the lance veered to the side and hit the post. It jerked back, knocking her brother clear off the saddle. He fell to the stones with a sickening, hollow thud.

She lunged forward but Thibaud held her back. She saw black rage bloom on her father's face.

Get up, Laurent. Get up.

Sunlight glinted off the dagger strapped to her father's belt as he strode to where her brother struggled up on his elbows. Through her mind flashed images of a beaten hound, a spitted squire, a wounded knight.

"Flesh of my flesh, unseated by a bag of grain," he muttered. "*This* is the son who remains to me."

Laurent managed to rise to his feet, reeling. He wiped his mouth with his sleeve and rasped, "I am no knight, father."

Her heart stopped.

"No, you are not." Her father swung his hand across Laurent's face, launching him to skid across the ground. "And you never will be."

Aliénor shouted her brother's name, jerking against Thibaud's grip, but her father turned his thunderous face toward her so fast that she froze.

"This crippled excuse of a boy," he said, turning to spit on the ground, "is no longer my heir."

Thibaud refused to release her until her father had strode across the courtyard, barking for wine, and the door to the donjon closed behind him. Racing to her brother, she fell to her knees. His eyes were just starting to open. Blood dripped from his nose, over his chin, and onto his tunic. She lifted the trailing ends of her tippet sleeves to wipe it away.

Her heart fluttered. "God's Blood, Laury, are you trying to get yourself killed?"

He winced as he pushed himself upright. "Knight's training has taught me how to fall off a horse without breaking my neck."

"Our father could have—"

"But he didn't." He jerked his head away from her fussing and instead swiped his sleeve across his mouth. "I'm alive, and everything is exactly as it should be."

"Are you out of your senses?" She sat back on her heels. "You know our father doesn't mean what he says when—"

"Yes, he does, and I'll hold him to it." His lips widened in a bloody grin. "You're the new heir, Ally. And I can finally join the monastery."

37

CHAPTER THREE

Jehan paced blindly in the nearly pitch-black cell. His head throbbed and tight stitching pulled the wound on his leg. The thick walls were cold and damp against his palm, yet he felt as hot as if he were walking in full armor on a sweltering summer afternoon.

He fought against the fever muddling his mind. He had to think clearly—too many people depended upon him now. Last year, when he'd breached the walls of Castétis and claimed it as his own, he'd promised his men-at-arms they'd never again have to return to their old, brutal life on the hills. And once the servants and vassals of Castétis had offered up their labor in exchange for his protection, he became as bound to them as they were to him.

He would live.

But to help them, he would have to escape.

He paused as he heard a voice outside his cell. He fixed his attention on the pale strip of light seeping in from under the door as shadows made it flicker. When the door swung open, light burst into the cell and hit his eyes like daggers. He squeezed them shut.

"I see you're feeling better."

He didn't need sight to recognize who'd arrived. This was the woman with hands as soft as velvet and a tongue as sharp as a knife. He'd been so feverish for so long he'd only been vaguely aware of her presence as a voice in the darkness, a touch in the night, and warmth when he shivered.

"How long have you been in the dark?" Dried rushes crackled as she moved around the room. "I'll bring you more candles next time."

A shadow passed across him as another person entered the cell. The man's grunts reminded Jehan that the maiden had a large, loyal servant as a guard.

She said, "Hugo, put the tray beside him."

A sliding noise was followed by the strong scent of charred meat and mustard sauce. Suddenly he was ravenous. He sank to the floor blindly, stretching out his injured leg so he wouldn't rip the stitches. He tilted his head toward the ground and dared to squeeze an eye open, shielding himself with a raised forearm against the light pouring in from the doorway. He seized the hunk of bread on the tray, ripping off a piece with his teeth as the boy stretched a cup into his sight. Jehan dropped the bread, grabbed the cup the boy was offering, and drank deeply.

As he gorged himself, his eyes adjusted to the light, degree by degree. The damp walls reflected the glimmer of two candles burning upon the single table. Rush light from the hall bathed the center of the cell in a square, reddish-orange glow. She stood framed by that glow, a slim silhouette, her hair capturing the firelight as loose, long curls tumbled over her shoulders. She bent over a sack, rummaging for something inside. The chain of her girdle hung away from her abdomen and its sway drew his attention to her narrow waist.

Dark thoughts scattered through his fevered mind. This daughter of Tournan had only a half-witted peasant and a single man-at-arms to guard her. Jehan knew he wasn't at his strongest, but desperation often gifted men with unexpected power. He could take her guards by surprise and subdue her. Then this daughter of Tournan would be his prisoner, a bargaining chip for his freedom.

He flexed his sore, swollen hand around the cup as a deeper instinct made him pause. She could be hurt in the scuffle, and most likely because of him. In his fever-weakness, he'd be clumsy and more forceful than needed. Sickness was clouding his thoughts. His vengeance should be aimed at her father, not at the woman who'd restored his life.

She approached him and knelt by his side, dangerously, he thought, considering the war going on in his head. She leaned so close that he smelled the scent of cardamom clinging to her clothes. She unwound the linen encircling his head. Her fingers probed the soreness on his temple.

She said, "You're still feverish."

He grunted around a mouthful of bread, "It will pass."

"Lucky for you," she said. "I believe it will."

She pressed a damp linen against his brow and the cold water stung the wound. After a while, she tossed the linen aside and started winding a fresh one around his head. Her pretty, pale face was as smooth as a mask, but even muddled by the spice-scent of her, he could see how the muscles of her throat stood out like cords.

He frowned. He wanted her beast of a father to be uneasy and anxious, not this woman. But since he was stuck in this cell, she was his only conduit to the viscount.

He asked, "How long have I been here?"

"Eight days."

"So long." He placed a burnt crust, all that was left of the bread, upon the tray. "The Prince of Wales will be at the gates any day now."

She laughed a short, humorless huff. "Eight *days*, not eight weeks, Sir Jehan. I suspect the news of your capture has not yet reached England."

"It need go no farther than Bordeaux, where the prince is gathering an army."

She rose up on her knees to tie the ends of the linen bandage secure. "It's foolish to try to frighten me."

"I'm speaking the truth. I'd received word of his arrival on the day your father captured me."

Her little nostrils flared. "How proud you must be, to think your liege lord would drop all other responsibilities to free a single knight."

"He will not take my capture or the death of my men lightly."

He saw her throat flex and knew that she'd finally heard what her father had done, though he was sure neither she nor her father yet understood the enormity of the implications.

"Since Castelnau has remained in my family's hands for two long centuries," she said, "I am not the least bit worried." She tugged on his worn, bloody shift. "Take this off."

He eased away from the wall and then pulled the linen garment over his head before tossing it to where some dirty hay formed his pallet.

She turned her head this way and that, staring at his naked abdomen, bare above the waist of his linen braies. "Your bruises are finally fading."

"No ribs broken."

"And no injuries inside, apparently. But you must stay very still nonetheless. And your hand?"

He raised it to the light, turning it so she could see how much less swollen it was than before.

"I'll survive now." He dropped his hand and reached for a leg of fowl as well as a change of subject. "Why hasn't your father sent me an envoy to raise the issue of ransom?"

"Be glad." She leaned over his injured thigh, one long tress slipping over her shoulder to brush across his braies.

His stomach muscles clenched. "I don't relish spending weeks in this cell."

"Consider yourself fortunate. He's not in the right state of mind for diplomacy."

"Nor murder, since I live still." But she was killing him in her own way, as that tress made tickling circles near his crotch.

"I didn't think you'd be so eager to hand over Castétis, Sir Jehan."

"I'm not." He tossed the bone on the tray as he spoke around a mouthful of chicken. "I'd rather die from starvation first."

She settled a level glare upon him. "If the way you're eating is any measure, I doubt you'd choose starvation."

Then Jehan saw himself reflected in her steady gaze, wearing nothing but his braies, eating like a beast, his chest covered with crumbs, and scowling at her. The ladies of the court at Bordeaux would swoon in fear rather than desire if they could see him now— yet this woman had the temerity to raise a brow.

He reacted by reflex. He didn't really know why he did it, but suddenly he plunged his good hand in her thick, warm hair, watching himself do it with a measure of surprise. She startled but did not jerk away. He searched her features for similarity to her father so he would have reason to dislike her, but he lost his intent as her dewy lips parted, as her breath rushed between her white teeth, as the skin-warmed perfume of the woman rose up from the gape in her kirtle to make a muddle of his thinking again. Her eyes were like gilded brown velvet. Her skin had the dewy texture of a young peach.

The half-wit was on his feet and the guard had pulled his sword, but she waved a hand to ward them off.

"You're feverish, Sir Jehan." Her gaze was as steady as that of a tournament knight across a jousting field. "Release me so I can see to your leg wound."

"You should fear me."

"I know how weak you are."

"You would be the perfect instrument of my vengeance."

"I saved your life."

"To make up for the murder of my men, my young squire?"

"Nothing ever will." A flutter of remorse crossed her face. "But my father's men tell me you're a chivalrous knight, despite your thievery."

Thievery.

The word plunged as deep as any dagger and made him loosen his grip. Her hair slipped through his fingers like silk. She couldn't possibly know how he'd spent his years before bending a knee to the Prince of Wales. He wasn't proud of the things he'd done on the hills of Gascony when he'd had only a sword and a good, if tattered, name. Chivalry wasn't a code that leant well to survival, but he'd put all that behind him.

He said, "What's this talk about thievery?"

"Isn't it obvious?" She gestured for the guard and the boy to ease their stances and then flung open a sack by her side. "You stole my dowry lands."

"I gained Castétis fairly, by force of arms." He couldn't deny he'd known that the house of Tournan had some claim upon Castétis, but when he seized it, it had been all but abandoned. "No one was guarding it. No one came to defend it—"

"My father was away." She pulled an earthenware bowl from the sack and peeled off the cloth cover. "He was lending his sword to an aristocratic family in Florence. Is it chivalrous to wait until the shepherd is sleeping to steal the sheep?"

No more chivalrous, he thought, than abandoning a castle and its people. He wouldn't easily forget the way those hungry villagers fell to their knees before him, as the first person who'd staked a claim. As she slathered some unguent across the wound on his leg, he wondered if she knew how bad the situation was. He suspected she didn't. A woman who would nurse her worst enemy in the hope of recovering her dowry wasn't the kind of woman who would suffer such negligence.

Then a new thought pinched him. "Is your father bargaining to find you a husband yet, with my lands as your dowry?"

She drew into herself like a whelk into its shell.

"So he is," he murmured. The viscount was ill-informed if he thought Jehan would give the castle up so easily.

"He has sent out messages." She dipped her fingers into the unguent again.

"Who is he considering?"

She canted her head at him, eyes narrowing in suspicion.

"It's been a long war between our kings," he explained. "I've met many Gascon knights loyal to the French king during truce negotiations with the prince. Over those weeks, a lot of wine is swilled and a lot of stories swapped. I might be able to tell you if your father's choice is a fool or an ogre."

"Are those my only choices?"

"Be glad you *have* choices." He gestured toward the damp walls of the cell. "Some of us have none."

"Oh, but you do have a choice, Sir Jehan. You can buy your freedom by giving me my castle."

"Well played." He felt the corners of his lips twitching. "As for these potential husbands…?"

She gave her head a shake. "The only reason you're asking me is so you will know who to battle to steal my castle away again."

"Your father didn't raise a fool."

"It won't be so easy next time." Her satiny shoulder pressed against the neckline of her kirtle. "I'll be at Castétis, securing it along with my future husband."

"Who will be…?"

"Persistent, aren't you?" She scraped her glistening fingers clean against the edge of the earthenware bowl. "I suppose there's no harm. My father makes no secret about what families he wishes to make alliances with. Theobald de Coysset is one possibility. So is Bernardi d'Aure."

"I've met them both, briefly."

"What about the Viscount de Baste?"

"He's old." *And lecherous.*

"He has three sons. I suspect I'll be offered a younger son, but my father has pinned his hopes on Guy, the oldest. Are you acquainted with the family?"

"I know Sir Guy, yes."

He did his best to mask his surprise. Theobald and Bernardi were good men, strong knights, with the same loyalties to King Jean as Aliénor's father. But Guy de Baste was another matter. Though the current Viscount de Baste was loyal to the French king, his son Guy was actively, if surreptitiously, seeking better relations with the English crown.

Jehan wondered if Aliénor's father was aware of this shifting of allegiances and realized, just as swiftly, that he couldn't be.

"Struck dumb, are you?" She set the pot aside and unfurled a clean length of linen. "Is Guy de Baste such a formidable opponent, then?"

"The ladies think him handsome, but he's an indifferent fighter."

"You'll forgive me if I doubt you." She slipped the linen under his leg to begin the winding, exposing a shadowy gap between her neckline and the lovely breasts beneath. "Knights seem to enjoy diminishing other knights' valor, if for no other reason than to glow in comparative virtue."

He didn't answer. He was still contemplating Guy de Baste's many insufficiencies. The man preferred to talk and bargain rather than to fight. He was glib with words, wore a cut of clothes straight out of court, and had all the slippery charm of a peddler of looted goods. Worst of all, he could be a conspirator of the worst sort, playing a very dangerous game. Any woman deserved a better fate than to bed a traitor.

It was an unsettling, fever-bidden thought.

"The next time I come, I'll take out the stitches." She pushed back on her heels. "For now, I've been gone too long."

"Wait."

He seized a handful of cloth as she stood up. It turned out to be a long, tapering sleeve hanging from above her elbow. It slid through his fingers as she straightened to her full height but he squeezed tighter to capture the tip.

He said, "I owe you my thanks."

Back-lit as she was by the rush light pouring through the door, he couldn't read her expression. "I've done no more," she said, "than what is expected of a noble house."

"What nobility resides in this house comes only from you, Aliénor. I know the true nature of your father."

She glanced away, toward the hallway. "Please don't insult my family, Sir Jehan. You know nothing about us."

"I make you the exception." He tried very hard to not notice the sweet indentation of her spine or the flare of her kirtle over the curve of her hips. "For that, I insist you don't return here anymore."

"Don't be foolish. The stitches need to be removed, and—"

"Send a servant in your place. I won't have your punishment on my conscience."

"Your conscience?" Her back straightened a measure. "Where was your conscience on the day you destroyed my future?"

He met those brown eyes, not as soft as before, and thought of the castle that had lifted him out of the life of a sell-sword, put the first real roof over his head in nearly a decade, and brought a measure of security long denied to him and to his men. Then he thought of the blood spilled in the name of Castétis, for no reason other than rage.

He let go of her tapering sleeve. "I mean you no harm, mademoiselle."

"But you harmed me anyway." She turned away only to stop in the portal, her hand on the doorjamb. "If you truly wish to thank me, Sir Jehan, then give me back my dowry."

CHAPTER FOUR

"When we reach the top of the hill," Laurent said, kicking his horse past her on the rocky slope, "you must keep to the edge of the woods."

Aliénor frowned at her brother's tone of voice. Had he forgotten he was her *younger* sibling? "Why bother? I'd rather ride in the open field."

"We'll need quick cover if we spot trouble." His head swiveled as he eyeballed the clearing on the height, the horizon beyond, and Castelnau on the hill behind them. Then he turned to her, his gaze filled with challenge. "But there's an open field between here and there, if you're game."

"You know I can't race," she began, but it was too late. Laurent had bent over the neck of his horse and now tore across the open field. The dogs, baying and wagging their tails, darted ahead of him, anxious to reach cover where they would sniff among the underbrush for rabbits and thrushes.

She rode in his wake a bit more sedately, one gloved hand aloft. Her sparrow hawk perched upon her wrist, the brass bells on the bird's legs jangling. In the breeze of the horse's pace, the hawk worried with her wings and opened her beak where it protruded from the feathered leather hood.

"Hah," Laurent said as Aliénor joined them by the edge of the woods. "I beat you again."

"It was no race," she retorted, lifting her arm higher. "I can't gallop with my bird on my arm."

"Excuses," he said, grinning. "At least she's getting used to the horse and the dogs."

"Finally."

"But shouldn't she be on a lure by now?"

"Soon enough, Laurent. Soon enough."

The sparrow hawk had been a gift from her father, brought home from Florence. She loved the way the hawk puffed out her soft chest and stared at her with intelligence in her light yellow eyes. There were times when she was tempted to release the creature from the ramparts rather than train her to the lure. It hurt her heart a little to see such a wild thing tethered and imprisoned.

Like the knight.

She frowned and shifted her seat on her mare. She hadn't seen the prisoner for a full fortnight, sending her maidservant to deliver food, candles, and drink in her stead. If Margot's reports were to be believed, Sir Jehan was growing ever stronger and more restless in his cell. It didn't seem right to imprison any creature within four stone walls. Even her hawk, though kept mostly in the mews, still had light and air and the companionship of several other birds. Yet despite his situation, Sir Jehan always sent his compliments with Margot, thanking "the daughter of the house" for seeing to his needs in defiance of her own father.

It might have been better if he'd remained angry, boastful and unrepentant. She had been on surer footing when she'd despised him.

"I'm taking you back," Laurent said, drawing his horse to a halt as a pine-scented breeze swept up over the cliff. "We've gone too far as it is."

Aliénor rolled her eyes. To think she taught this boy to tie his own braies.

"I wonder," Laurent said, tipping his chin toward the far horizon, "if the Prince of Wales' army is just beyond the far ridge."

"Don't be fanciful. It's too late in the season for the prince to start marching around with an army."

"The Prince of Wales didn't come all the way to Bordeaux just to play dice with his English vassals."

"But sending an army through Gascony makes no sense. The harvest is in, and soon the cold rains will come. He'll have nothing to feed his knights, and any siege will have to be done through a long winter."

"Father's taking the threat seriously, though. I'm sure you've noticed."

She met his grimace with one of her own. Her father's mood was the reason they'd saddled up for a ride. The atmosphere in the castle was growing tenser with every passing day. Her father barked orders at the men-at-arms who had to take shifts to keep an all-day and all-night watch on the ramparts. The maidservants skittered about with bowed shoulders. Even the hounds cowered. After her father's two-year absence, she'd almost forgotten how angry and disruptive his presence could be to the peaceful rhythms of castle life she made such efforts to maintain.

She turned her horse toward the path and kicked her into a trot along the line of the woods. "Talk to me of some more pleasant subject, Laurent."

"I'll tell you about the abbey in Toulouse."

She gave him a frown from beneath the rim of her pointed hunting cap. "Still dreaming of a cold cell?"

"I'm still disinherited."

"Laurent, you know that could change in the blink of an eye."

"Then I will have earned this for nothing." He tapped the scar on his chin from the wound he received on the day their father dispossessed him.

She wondered how deep that scar went, and whether it had a twin on his heart.

"The chaplain told me," Laurent continued, in as bright a voice as before, "many of the monks teach at the university in Toulouse. Often, they take pilgrimages. To Avignon to see the Pope, to shrines all over France, even as far as Rome…"

As Laurent chattered on, her heart sank. She knew she would rarely see him once he entered the monastery. She couldn't imagine the castle without his presence. In the early years, when she used to return home from the convent for holidays, Laurent had followed her around like a bird with a broken wing. She'd watched him smile his first smile—certainly, it seemed like his first—when she'd presented him with his own pup, a fine greyhound from a litter they'd watched being born. Mostly, as the years progressed and plague stole their family away, she'd hidden him from their father whenever she anticipated one of his rages.

Laurent was the last of her siblings.

If she lost him, she would be alone.

She interrupted his story by lunging for the reins of his horse. "Promise me," she said, pulling him to a stop, "that you won't leave Castelnau until I'm wed."

His brows disappeared behind the flop of his hair. "You'll be married soon, I expect. All those messages father has sent—"

"All the more reason to promise."

"I'll do so willingly, *sor.*" He bent his head. "I won't leave Castelnau, not until I've had a glass of wine at your wedding."

Halfway through the sign of the cross, Laurent went still. After a moment, he cocked his head toward the woods.

"Laurent, what are you—"

"Hush."

He seized his reins back and kicked his mount ahead. Then he cut sharply in front of her mare. Her mare huffed and high-stepped backwards as Laurent used his own steed's greater mass to force both beasts deeper into the shadow of a stone outcropping.

Only then did she hear, with rising alarm, the muffled thudding of horses' hooves and the rising jangle of spurs, chain mail, and armor. The noise came from the woods somewhere ahead of them, closer to the path, cutting them off from their only route home.

Her brother glanced over his shoulder, all whites-of-eyes, his jaw tight. For one strange, blurry moment he looked exactly like their father. He raised a finger to his lips then scraped his sword out of the scabbard.

Her heart tumbled. He was protecting her, this little brother of hers, but in a stomach-dropping flash, she remembered every one of his heartbreaking, half-hearted sword-fighting lessons that had left him flat on his back on the paving stones.

She startled when the first riders burst out of the camouflage of the trees. She strained to see beyond Laurent's bodily shield, counting no more than six or eight mounted men. They rode hard toward the path on the slope, not sparing a single glance their way.

"Lower your sword, Laurent," she said, as she caught her breath.

"I will not." He raised it. "I'll protect you."

"They are no threat to us." She ran her fingers over her wind-tousled hair. "My future in-laws have arrived."

***

Aliénor headed down the stairs of the castle, smoothing the snug red and green *mi-parti* surcoat over her waist and abdomen. Around her hips, she wore a gold chain wound with a rope of pearls. She kept rolling those pearls under her palms as if the nubby sensation could calm her. She'd been like this all her life: Whenever her hopes were raised, equally so were her fears.

Her potential future father-in-law, the Viscount de Baste, had left early this morning after spending only a single day and night in the castle. She thought all had gone well as she presided over the meal yesterday afternoon, but his haste in leaving did not bode well, nor did the fact that none of his sons had accompanied him on this visit.

She knew this was all foolishness born of silly kitchen-servant talk and the sly side-eye of superstitious villagers, but maybe the de Bastes had heard about her last two betrothals ending in the deaths of her future bridegrooms. The first one had died eight years ago on the battlefield at Crécy, and the second one had died six years ago during the plague. Maybe de Baste thought the absence of his sons might serve as a shield against the death-curse of a woman twice engaged but never married.

Such idiocy. She grunted to herself and shook the thoughts out of her head as she entered the great hall. Her father stood close to the huge fireplace, alone. A few men-at-arms lingered around the table, clutching cups of wine. Sir Rostand glanced up from honing his dagger and gave her an encouraging nod.

"Ah, my daughter." Her father approached, holding out both hands to her. "Come."

She crossed the distance to take his hands, trying not to read her future in the seriousness of his expression. But when she rose from her curtsey she couldn't help but notice his deepening frown.

He said, "How old are you now, Aliénor?"

"Twenty-three next Candlemas Day, my lord."

"How quickly the time passes." The slash he'd received in the battle with Sir Jehan glowed across his cheek and nose. "But it matters no more. You impressed our guests yesterday acting as the lady of the house. You even fooled the viscount into thinking you are a quiet and amenable creature."

Her smile didn't quite reach her cheeks. It had not been easy to play the docile, ignorant young girl to a beady-eyed viscount who kept staring at the gape in her kirtle every time she served him wine.

He said, "You've guessed, no doubt, that I've found a husband for you."

She startled, then blurted, "Who?"

"The viscount's firstborn son, Guy, as I'd hoped. Someday you will become the lady of Baste as well as the lady of Tournan."

Her heart lifted and fell all at once, for though the betrothal meant she'd never step foot in a convent, her father's last words also confirmed he'd dispossessed Laurent for good.

"Have I not done well for you, daughter?"

She forcibly brightened her countenance. "I'm surprised, father. I didn't think…since Guy de Baste did not join his father in visiting—"

"His eldest son was kept away by his duties in the court of King Jean."

"Of course," she stuttered, for the viscount had said so himself, "but our guests left so early this morning, I was sure there was no time to set terms."

"De Baste was eager to return to the safety of his castle, considering the rumors coming out of Bordeaux. But we've agreed to terms, quite satisfactory ones."

"Including Castétis?"

The question was a risk, but she couldn't bring herself to retract it even as a silence grew between them.

"Your dowry is my entire estate," he said, with irritation. "I made that exceedingly clear to you and your wretched brother."

"Forgive me. For so long, Castétis was all I hoped for."

"Then it's fortunate you no longer have to hang your hopes upon it, daughter. It may take years to get it back."

"Years?"

"The English knight says he prefers imprisonment."

Her heart stuttered a beat. "You've spoken to Sir—to the prisoner?"

"Three weeks ago he was all but dead." Her father tilted his head to glower at her. "Now I'm told he rises, sleek and well-tended. Resurrected like the son of God."

"But isn't it fortunate," she said, her tongue with a will of its own, "that he still lives to trade his freedom as ransom for Castétis?"

"And yet a weakened knight would be easier to bargain with than one full of defiance and obstruction."

"You are wise as always, but I wonder at what shame would fall upon our house if he died in our cell—"

"He brought this on his own head."

"Of course," she persisted, "but mother always taught me that men of noble blood, even prisoners, aren't usually...confined in a cell. They're welcome at table, given the run of the castle on their honor—"

"This man has no honor."

She knew that tone, so she let her lashes fall over her eyes. Her gaze settled on her father's soft leather boots, planted wide upon the flagstones. His disapproval seemed to heat the veil upon her hair, but she knew well enough a lowered gaze and a dipped chin could work wonders.

So did plain good sense, when presented as if he'd figured it out himself.

"Perhaps," she ventured, taking a breath in anticipation of an angry lecture, "the prisoner is like the sparrow hawk you gifted me, father."

She took some solace in her father's silence, even if it made the air feel as dense as stone.

"In the beginning," she continued, "when I tethered her in the mews, she bit at her jesses and screeched at me and clawed herself bloody."

"You must be more firm with the bird," he snapped.

"But she has stopped all that now. All she really wanted was to be set free within the mews, to explore and move around. Once I began giving her daily exercise in the open air, she became as tame as could be."

Her father turned the cup of wine in his hands, squinting at her with a frown.

"Granted, I'm still working on the lure," she conceded, "but the hawk listens to my commands. She's so much calmer, now that she has a small measure of freedom."

Her father grunted and took a deep sip of his wine. When he lowered the cup, his gaze shifted to some point beyond the walls. She could all but see her suggestion taking root in his mind.

"Indeed," he said, returning his attention to her. "I have chosen the wisest of my children to be my heir."

She bowed her head.

"But if the thief ever wishes to be truly free," he warned, "he'd better fly to my lure sooner rather than later."

CHAPTER FIVE

God's Bones, it felt good to be out of that damn cell.

Guided out of the northwest tower by a guard, Jehan paused as he emerged into the sunshine, eyes closed against the brightness of the morning. He smelled loamy moss, the metallic scent of stone, and the tartness of a recent rain. He heard the huff of horses coming from a nearby stable and leather scuffing across the paving stones of the courtyard. The muffled voices of men drifted down from the ramparts as the scent of cooking meat wafted past, along with a heated wind that could only come from the kitchens.

He drew in a breath, expanding his lungs until he felt like his bruised chest would burst. When a clinking of chain mail alerted him to an approaching knight, he opened his eyes.

"A circuit of the courtyard is permitted," the knight barked, "if your wounds allow."

Jehan met Sir Rostand's frowning gaze. Jehan had been introduced to this knight a week ago in his cell, when the viscount had sent his burly vassal as an envoy in a vain effort to negotiate ransom. "Wounds or no wounds," Jehan said, "I'll circle this place a dozen times over."

"Stay within the walls," Rostand warned. "Don't do anything so foolish that it will force me to draw a sword."

"As I told you before, my fight is not with you."

"Nonetheless," Sir Rostand said, "my fealty to my liege lord requires me to act if you bolt for the open gate."

Jehan raised a brow as he cocked his wounded leg to better show the stitches through the rent in his hose. "Put a guard on me if you think you must."

"Not giving an inch, are you?" Rostand's frown deepened. "An honorable knight would swear not to escape—"

"—except a viscount with no honor deserves none in return."

No doubt Sir Rostand would have said more, but Jehan had already glanced past him, distracted by a far finer sight.

Aliénor emerged from the round central tower dominating the courtyard. With hounds dancing about her feet, she skimmed down the stairs as light as a leaf. She was more petite and willowy than he remembered, a slim pip of a woman in a dark blue woolen kirtle. She stopped and glanced his way when he shouted her name.

He took a step in her direction but Sir Rostand slapped a hand on his shoulder. "Be wise," the knight warned. "There isn't a man in this castle who wouldn't cut you in half if you harmed one hair on her head."

"She is safe in my presence." He glared until the knight removed his hand. "I owe her my life."

He headed her way, feeling the wound on his leg tug with each limping step. She waited with the hounds leaping around her feet as her brown eyes widened. He figured he must cut a gruesome figure, dressed in his battered surcoat that still bore bloodstains no laundresses could apparently pound out. He stopped a slight span away from her, so as not to make her fearful.

He said, "I'd wager my sword it's you who's responsible for freeing me from my cell."

She stood like a young deer ready to bolt. "I had little to do with it, Sir Jehan."

"You're a terrible liar." He held out his hand. "If you will permit me, I will give honor to the one who deserves it."

She hesitated, looking askance at his hand. "You're trying to start trouble." She glanced over her shoulder toward the donjon. "If my father should see you thus—"

"I shall tell him I was overcome by your beauty."

"Then he'll toss you back in the cell for good."

"It's a risk I'm willing to take."

He spread his palm wider. Narrowing her gaze, she hesitated for another moment before stepping forward to slip her hand into his. Lowering his head, he pressed his lips against the back of her hand. A shivering little current shuddered through her fingers. He breathed in a resinous perfume clinging to her skin, like she'd spent the morning spinning thread from fresh lambs-wool. He resisted a sudden, hungry urge to follow the trail of the scent with his lips.

He let her fingers slip out of his palm and then linked his hands behind his back, locking his fingers together tight. "It's a fine thing to see you in the bright of day, mademoiselle."

"That's enough of playing the troubadour." A little frown-line deepened between her brows. "We are not friends, Sir Jehan."

"I would change that."

"Don't be foolish."

"I can't be your enemy if I'm in your debt, little dove."

One fair, winged brow shot up at the endearment. "Shall I get you parchment and ink, sir, to write your pretty words?"

He shrugged. "A sword would do me better."

"For escape, it certainly would. I heard you've made no pledge to my father."

"But I'd make you one, if I had a sword. A pledge of protection."

"It's not your protection I need—or your friendship." She bent slightly to run a hand over the head of a begging hound. "It's Castétis, which my father tells me you still refuse to give up."

He smiled a slow smile that made her defiant expression melt into confusion.

"What?" she said.

"Congratulations are in order, I hear."

She raised her hands to her hips, frustrating the hounds begging for her favor. "And what gossip has reached your ears, you so deep in your cell?"

"You've been made your father's heir. In which case, Castétis should mean nothing to you now."

"So Margot has been delivering gossip as well as food." Her gaze slid away. "I thought she was too fearful of you to chatter."

Jehan didn't deny it, though Margot wasn't the source of his information. He figured there was no reason to get Sir Rostand in the bad graces of this woman, for the guilt-ridden knight had told him much during the short time they'd spent in his cell.

"It's still my dowry, you know." Her chin tilted a fraction. "Castétis."

"But not as vital to your happiness or your future as before."

"My father could change his mind with a shift in the wind, leaving me in the same situation as before." Her jaw tightened as if she were ashamed to have spoken so. "In any case, you stole something, so you should return it. Nobody likes a thief."

The word was a kick to the gut. He'd spent too many years trying to erase all those dark years of thievery to let her cast that dark shadow over him without challenge. "Then ask me," he said, tossing the command like a gauntlet. "Ask me why I seized your castle."

She shrugged. "I can only assume it was greed."

"Have you ever been to Castétis?"

"As a girl, before the plague." She turned her face away to glance up at the sky, scudding with clouds. "I used to run barefoot through the garden of my uncle's house. I played in the stream and caught frogs and slept in a big bed piled in with all my cousins. Once you surrender it, I will journey there again with my brother and—"

"It's no longer fit for a lady."

"I know it's no grand chateau."

"When I seized it, it was half in ruins. The roof was a sieve. Pigs had the run of the courtyard. The northeast wall was crumbling. My men and I had to do no more than climb over the wall in the night."

A ripple of uncertainty passed across her face. "If that's true," she ventured, "then it should be no matter to you to give it up."

"Except Castétis is everything I possess."

With a heady rush he remembered the day he'd climbed over the chemise wall with his sword raised and made Castétis his own. The castle was in shambles, yes, but he could see it, repaired and strong, in his mind's eye, solid enough to last generations. Castétis was the first *real* boon he'd received from his position as the prince's man, for though the Prince of

Wales had made extravagant promises of great English wealth and lands, Jehan had yet to see a single fruit of those wild assurances.

Aliénor frowned at him with a little knot between her brows, ignoring the laundress wading through the dogs with her arms piled with linens, and the shouts of two boys chasing each other across the paving stones.

"Even if Castétis is everything you possess," she said, "wouldn't you willingly give it up in exchange for your freedom?"

"No." He shook his head. "I've had freedom without land before, and I nearly starved because of it."

He watched her expression, hoping for a glimmer of understanding, seeing only confusion and suspicion and, by the tightness of her chin, a growing resistance to listen anymore. He supposed this daughter of a viscount, in her fine kirtle and belt of gold links, had never been poor, hungry, or desperate. In any case, it was becoming clear that discussing the castle he'd stolen from her wasn't the wisest way to curry her good opinion.

For reasons he did not dare to examine too deeply, he very much intended to win this lady's favor.

So, determined to steer the conversation in a different direction, he crouched as well as he could, stretching out his hurt leg, and held out a hand to the most rambunctious of the hounds. The pup darted toward him, jumping onto his bent knee to aim a wet tongue at his face.

He let the pup get a few licks in before holding him away to riffle his ears. "This one bears a strong resemblance to a hunter my grandfather used to own," he said. "Same long snout, same rusty brown coat, same amber eyes. Maybe this pup is one of his line. Does it belong to your kinsman Thibaud?"

"No," she said flatly. "All the hounds belong to my father."

"They knew each other, you know." He squinted up at her against the bright sun. "Thibaud and my grandfather, the Baron of St. Simon."

"Oh?" She was watching him handle the pup with an odd look on her face. "I suppose I shouldn't be surprised. If half his tales are true, Thibaud has known every nobleman from here to the English sea."

He enjoyed the view of her hair haloed in the rosy light of the morning. "Back when your great-uncle and my grandfather knew one another," he said, "the barony of St. Simon was equal in power to the Tournans—"

"Until the Count of Armagnac gobbled up your lands."

He raised a brow in surprise.

"As well as telling outrageous stories, Thibaud gives history lessons," she explained, clicking her tongue as a dog wandered off, drawn to a pigeon landing upon the stable-eaves.

"Did Sir Thibaud tell you he battled against my grandfather's forces twenty years ago—"

"Wait," she interrupted. "So they were enemies?"

"Yes."

A confused little laugh slipped out of her. "Sir Jehan, if you're trying to encourage kinder relations between us, you might have chosen a better example."

"They're the perfect example." Her laugh raised his hopes as well as a lovely flush on her cheeks. "Thibaud and my grandfather were the kind of enemies who embraced each other at tournaments and shared war stories over pitchers of new wine."

"I've witnessed such behavior many a time," she said, shaking her head. "I've never understood it."

"Loyalties may diverge, but knights respect one another anyway."

The corner of her mouth twitched. "But I am not a knight, Sir Jehan."

"Thankfully so," he said, resisting the urge to run his gaze from the tip of her slippers to the pink-tinged curve of her ears. "Yet I'm certain you'll understand why a knight with nothing but a good name and a fine sword makes desperate choices."

She lifted a brow. "Like becoming the vassal of the Prince of Wales and stealing castles from unsuspecting maidens?"

"Being the prince's vassal," he said pointedly, "was a better living than selling my sword to the highest bidder, which I did for three long years before

I met the prince."

The smile disappeared from her face and that's how he knew he'd made a mistake. God knows what he was doing, spilling his shame to this dagger-tongued sylph of a girl.

"Sir Jehan, you baffle me. Sell-swords have harried the villagers for years. They wound my father's men, steal the harvest—"

"They are forced to do so when war wanes, because noblemen release them to avoid feeding them. The only other option is starvation."

The look she gave him was half confusion and half exasperation. So he eased the pup off his knee and rose to his full height. "My point," he said, wishing he could slip his fingertips across her delicate collarbone, "is that we are both subject to the wills and wars of our liege lords. That's the reason we've both been dispossessed, in different measures. Why should we hate each other just because our liege lords say we are enemies?"

She held up her chin like a dare. "And how kindly do you feel toward those men who seized your grandfather's title and land?"

"Not kindly at all. But I had no choice, no more than those men who did their lord's bidding."

"I know what it is like," she blurted, her throat flexing, "to have no choice at all. Indeed, I've felt like that my whole life."

Her little nostrils flared. For a moment, he thought she was going to say something more, but she tightened her lips and started to tug at her own hands, as if twisting invisible rings around her fingers.

"Then you understand," he said softly, "why I took Castétis."

She said nothing, but her head moved in such a way that he imagined she meant it for acknowledgment.

"I did not know it was yours," he said. "All I saw was a castle neglected, and a bright future within my grasp. So I seized it with both hands."

She hazarded a glance up at him. In that space, a current of mutual understanding rushed between them, a sense of communion thrumming like the ringing of a church bell. He curled his fingers into his palms so he wouldn't grip her by those lovely shoulders and bring her sweet face closer to his. In the pause he realized that the whole of the courtyard had hushed along with them. He'd been so keen on putting forth his argument that he hadn't noticed the attention they'd garnered from kitchen maids, stable boys, and men-at-arms alike, all while he and Aliénor stood across from each other with the dogs circling their feet, talking as if no one else existed.

That attention prevented him from tracing the little line deepening between her brows, or slipping a finger under the curve of her chin and tilting her face up so she would look at him, really *look* at him with those soft brown eyes. Instead, he stood as still as a watch guard while his blood warmed, willing this singular woman to bestow her favor upon him.

"I'm off to fetch my hawk, Sir Jehan." She twisted on a heel before casting a shy glance over her shoulder. "Would you be so kind as to accompany me while I exercise her in the courtyard?"

CHAPTER SIX

With the knight limping beside her, Aliénor crossed to the mews in a numb sort of daze, still thrumming with the intensity of their conversation. He'd parried all her objections, argued his point, and brushed off her barbs like dog hair from his hose. She struggled to reconcile her former opinion of him with the idea that he was simply a dispossessed knight struggling to control his own fate. More than their pace had harmonized, it seemed, as side-by-side they crossed the courtyard.

She left him outside the mews and slipped in through the narrow door to dive deep into the cross-hatched shadows. She sucked in the first full breath she'd managed since she'd glimpsed him looming in the courtyard. Her heart beat fast under the palm of her hand as she pressed her chest in a vain effort to slow it. She had to gather her wits quick or she'd make a fool of herself for sure.

She seized a boiled leather glove, unhooked the sparrow hawk's leash from the perch, and wound it about her own leather-bound wrist. She took her time coaxing the bird onto the glove before she dared to step back into the courtyard. Under Jehan's bold blue stare, her heart did yet another skitter-step.

Later, she told herself. When she was out of the power of his physical presence, she'd be able to think this all through more clearly.

"A fine-looking bird," he said, as he came around so he'd walk on the opposite side of her hawk. "Have you had her long?"

"She was a gift from my father." She spoke a low, firm word to her spaniel to stop jumping on her. "But perhaps we shouldn't talk about him."

"Or Castétis," he added wryly. "At least I know where the battle lines are drawn." He grinned a crooked sort of smile, the kind that made the back of her knees soften. "What of your mother? Is she off-limits for conversation?"

"No," she said. "My mother was from Normandy." With a pang, she thought about how much she could use a mother's advice now. "The French king arranged the marriage to my father to secure his loyalty."

"The northern heritage must explain the glory of your hair. There are few Gascons so fair."

She felt her cheeks heat at the compliment. "My mother's eyes were more worthy of envy—they were the shade of heather."

"Heather is common on the hills." His gaze strayed to the bird. "Your eyes are the shade of a hawk's plumage—brown with streaks of gold."

"Did I not warn you about playing the troubadour, Sir Jehan?"

"I speak only the truth."

"Troubadours don't speak truth. They sing romantic songs about unobtainable love to silly maidens who should know better."

His quick laugh was colored with surprise. "Some Abbess told you that."

"No, I figured it out myself." She suppressed a shudder at the memory of her cold cell. "Troubadours used to visit Castelnau, now and again, in the years when war waned, before the plague made travel dangerous."

"And you don't swoon when a troubadour sings?"

"There's only so much foolishness I can abide."

"In the court at Bordeaux, the ladies sigh over every song. What a singular woman you are, Aliénor."

She caught his eye and a heavy charge crackled between them, like the air when the black clouds of a summer storm came, dancing like sparks across her skin.

She turned her gaze away. "You would have saved me much misery if you'd become a troubadour. A lute is far less dangerous than a sword."

"It depends on what one wishes to capture. A

woman's heart, for example, is rarely captured at sword point."

"But a lute," she said pointedly, "cannot capture a castle or lands."

"It can, if the troubadour uses a lute to woo and win a woman who is in possession of such riches."

"But then you risk breaking the lady's heart for wanting her possessions more than her heart."

"Alas." He spread his palms upward. "Even a troubadour can't lure an heiress with empty hands."

Her glance fell to one of those hands, and the dirty bandage upon it, so she took the opportunity to veer to a less dangerous subject. "The swelling of your hand seems to have subsided."

"Then let me take off the bindings."

"And release you to wield your terrible weapons?"

"There's not a lute or sword within my reach, mademoiselle, and I don't think the guards will hand me either."

"I suppose it can do no harm," she said, though her heart said otherwise when he smiled again.

"Good! I am tired of spilling wine." Jehan yanked the end of the linen free, and then rapidly unwound the cloth. Once unbound, he flexed his fingers and turned his wrist, confirming to her the damage had been no worse than a sprain.

She said, "Any pain?"

"A bit stiff."

"You shouldn't raise a shield for a while, but it

looks healthy enough."

"Thanks to your skill. You'll make a fine wife someday."

"Someday," she said, "will be the feast of the Epiphany."

She'd blurted it like it was nothing and regretted it a moment later. She turned her gaze to the ramparts to better keep a hold on her wits, because every time she let her thoughts stray to the prospect of her wedding, her insides tightened up and her mind spiraled with anxious thoughts and she felt as if a great shadowed hand were coming down upon her.

He said, "Your father didn't waste any time."

"I'm nearly twenty-three years of age."

"You're in the flower of womanhood."

"Every girl I knew at the convent is married, one with five children at last count."

"Envious?"

"Of a manner." She made the mistake of glancing at him and seeing a flattering curiosity in his expression. "They've had the freedom of their own homes. They've become mistresses of their own castles and lives."

"Who is your lucky groom?"

She gave him a swift shake of her head. "I'm not sure I want to tell you."

"Then it must be Sir Guy."

She frowned at his all-too-accurate guess.

"If you wish," he offered, "I could describe him to you."

"Don't."

He raised a black brow.

"Knowing more will only disappoint me," she explained, as they passed the open portal and continued their circuit. "If you tell me Sir Guy is ungainly, uncouth, or oddly disfigured, I shall await my marriage with dread. And if you paint him as a fine young knight, I will dream up unreasonable expectations."

"You're not curious?"

"Of course I am. But marriage is a labor no matter what, isn't it?" For her mother, it was a heavy burden after Crécy, when her father became a hard man to live with. "But marriage is better than the alternative. I'd rather throw myself off the ramparts than join a nunnery."

"Indeed." His voice dropped. "You deserve a happy marriage, Aliénor, with the best match your father can manage."

She cast him a sharp glance, for there was no light poetry in his words this time. He avoided her eye to focus on the pattern of the paving stones as they walked. Even her sparrow hawk sensed the change in mood, flapping her wings with enough force to lift her half off the glove. Aliénor cooed soft words, doing her best to settle the bird while Jehan brooded.

Finally, curiosity and suspicion overcame her. She scuffed to a stop near the northwest tower. "Sir Jehan, if there is something you must tell me about my betrothed," she said, as the hawk's talons pierced the boiled leather glove, "then please do. And do it quickly, before my courage fails me."

He pivoted so he stood in front of her. His shadow fell upon her face, and the bright blue sky behind his head was echoed in the color of his eyes. He was no closer to her than before, not so physically close as to cause alarm, or draw undue attention from the men-at-arms in the courtyard, but she caught her breath anyway. She noticed the pattern of stubble on his cheek, the way the breeze ruffled his hair, the way he seized all her attention with the fervid intensity of his stare. The courtyard seemed to dissolve away while her focus narrowed to the powerful emotions in those eyes.

"Guy de Baste doesn't deserve you," he said. "Any man with red blood in his veins would kill to make you his own."

And suddenly there wasn't enough air in all of Gascony for her to breathe.

CHAPTER SEVEN

He might have stood there for hours, snared by the way her lower lip quivered, entranced by the blush stealing up her jaw. He might have stood for days, captivated by the way her shoulders shuddered with the swiftness of her breath. He might have stood there for weeks, on the faintest hope that she might allow him, with the slightest encouragement, to lower his head and press his lips against her mouth.

He would have happily stood there forever, indeed, if a shout hadn't come from the ramparts.

Shout followed shout and they were no longer the center of attention as the courtyard erupted in activity. Women hurried out of the goat and chicken pens, grain baskets on their hips, splattering mud as they flooded into the courtyard to see what was happening. Men-at-arms rose from their ease, emerging from the kitchens, the stables, and flooding through the door of the donjon.

Aliénor gave him a startled look before turning on a heel and all but flying away from him. He watched the slim curve of her back as she shot toward the mews and slipped inside. He stared at the mews' door, as fixated as her hounds, until she reemerged. He watched as she brushed paw prints off her kirtle and headed toward the stairs to the donjon. Only as she stepped up did Jehan notice her father descending the stairs to await the rider whose horse's hooves now clattered on the wooden drawbridge.

The messenger yanked his steed to a stop and all but fell out of the saddle, as drenched with sweat and mud as his mount. The man swayed as he made his bow. "My lord, mademoiselle," he said, heaving out a breath. "The Prince of Wales and his army are in Seissan."

Seissan.

Jehan's blood thundered in his ears. The walled village was less than a half-day's ride to the east.

His liege lord had come.

Jehan turned his face to the viscount, feeling the brightness of his own triumph, but the viscount didn't spare a look his way. The nobleman tossed a leg of fowl to the ground with such fury even the hounds hesitated to leap for it. Jehan stepped forward, determined that the murdering fool would see him and know *he* was the cause of the army soon to arrive at the gate—but then his gaze fell upon the woman by the viscount's side.

Unease tempered the heat of his triumph. As

much as he wanted the prince to rain fire and arrows upon her father, he didn't want Aliénor in the midst of it.

Jehan jerked as a guard seized his arm. He dug his feet into the stones when the guard yanked him back, no doubt toward the door to the northwest tower. Jehan then did what he should have been doing since he'd been released into the courtyard: He took a swift inventory of the barrels of arrows and oil and stones lying about, as well as the number of fighting men climbing to the ramparts.

"Rudel," Sir Rostand shouted, striding toward them from the stables. "Leave Sir Jehan to me. You'll take the first shift on the wall-walk."

His guard said, "I'll put him in his cell first—"

"I'll escort the prisoner to the cell." Rostand waved his hand toward the ramparts. "Now go."

As Rudel headed for the stairs, Jehan eyed the thick-bearded Sir Rostand with sudden, but cautious, interest. The burly knight cast an emotionless gaze over his shoulder at the courtyard—made chaotic as servants raced out the portal to gather their families and possessions from the village below. Once Aliénor's father had climbed the stairs to the ramparts and was out of sight, Sir Rostand casually walked past the door to the northwest tower and continued to walk on a path paralleling the main rampart wall.

Curious, Jehan followed Sir Rostand to the far side of the central tower, an isolated place under an arched awning. As the knight turned, his sword clattered against the plate armor. Jehan crouched into a fighting stance, his heart leaping.

"Stand *down*," Sir Rostand hissed. "Our time is brief."

Jehan didn't lower his fists. He wouldn't put it past Tournan to have him murdered and make it look like an escape attempt to save his tattered honor. But Sir Rostand made no move for his sword. Instead the black-bearded knight glanced around the narrow area with unease.

"I represent myself and two others," he said. "Sir Geoffrey of Garrigas and Sir David de Bourreu. They, like me, took no part in what happened the day you were captured."

His thoughts darkened. "Yet my squire and three of my men are dead."

"I can do nothing for your dead now except pray for their souls."

This knight had told him as much when he'd arrived in the cell with a jug of new wine and a troubled brow. "You bring me words, Sir Rostand, but your mistress showed more courage than all of you."

"Yon maiden is the only living creature who can tame the beast of her father. Do you want to hear our offer or don't you?"

"Speak."

"Tournan is our liege lord. We cannot openly defy him lest we lose our land and be branded traitors."

Jehan nodded. He understood the importance of vows of fealty better than Sir Rostand would ever know.

"If the prince comes," the knight continued, "we will fight him, according to our sacred oath."

"If the prince comes, you will lose."

"Perhaps that is true," Rostand said, and the skin above his beard darkened. "And perhaps it's not. We have high walls, enough men, and time on our side. But I don't relish the prospect of a long, hard siege."

Jehan resisted the urge to contradict him. The prince wouldn't suffer sitting around waiting to starve out the inhabitants of some small castle. The prince certainly hadn't done that for the bastide of Seissan, a walled village that should have been able to hold off an army for months at a time. This English prince liked to win his battles by boldness, burning, and extreme force—and frequently in ways few warriors expected.

"To avoid a siege," Rostand said, "I can think of only one solution: If you escape, there'll be no need for a conflict."

At the word *escape* the world opened up before Jehan's eyes, as if the walls themselves dissolved around him to reveal the rolling sweep of land and the great vineyards beyond, and for a moment it was as if he were on a racing steed flying free from here, free from the viscount, with Aliénor's blonde hair streaming across his face.

No.

Impossible.

"Decide quickly," Sir Rostand urged, "before we are discovered."

"What price for this freedom?"

"A promise to ward off your prince," he said. "Ask him to spare the village, the fields, this castle and all within it. With you returned alive and healthy, your English prince can go off and seek easier quarry because he will have already won what he came here for."

Jehan's chest constricted so he felt the soreness of every bruise. Vengeance was not an easy thing to surrender when he'd had so much time to nurture it in a cold dungeon cell.

"Lady Aliénor saved your life," Sir Rostand reminded him. "If you will not do this for me and my fellows, then at least do it for her."

Jehan breathed hard, his fists flexing, imagining the prince's army pouring over the ramparts, into the courtyard, into her room.

"I'll ask the prince," he said, as doubt crept along the edges of his determination. "But I cannot promise you he will listen."

"If you do not try, then there's no hope at all."

*****

He'd escaped!

With Hugo's help, Aliénor rolled out a new wine cask, an excuse to do something other than wince at the shouts and raised voices coming from the great hall. She'd herded all the servants inside the buttery to get them away from the hail of cups, jugs, serving trays, and food her father flung about in his inchoate rage. Now she could only hope Sir Rostand had enough strength left in him to ward off her father's fury, for when the big knight had come stumbling, bloody and half-conscious, into the hall, the look her father had lain upon him had made her blood go cold.

Escaped!

She should be furious, she thought, as she wrestled the wooden bung from the cask of wine with trembling hands. Jehan had seen the defenses of the castle and knew the extent of their preparations. Setting the tap, she picked up a hand-mallet and fixed it firm with a few double-handed hits. Maybe Jehan had played her for a fool as he'd squired her around the courtyard, no doubt taking count of men-at-arms while distracting her with conversation. Maybe from the very first he'd meant to escape without ever surrendering her castle at all.

I saw a bright future within my grasp so I seized it with both hands.

Yes, he'd seized an opportunity, and for that she should be despairing. But she didn't dare put a label on these strong, shivering feelings coursing through her—as if she herself were escaping to freedom along with him, her heart like a kestrel cut free of its jesses.

Bewildered, she turned her mind to the easier task at hand. "Heft the cask into the rack, Hugo," she ordered. The boy-man lifted the wine cask like it was a pillow, then, once the barrel was settled, she turned the tap and caught the golden flow in a jug. She was halfway through filling the second jug when she noticed the silence.

Closing the tap, she set both jugs upon the table and hurried to peek into the mead hall, flinging out a hand to keep the servants from tumbling into the room. Except for the furious swirling of dust motes in the light streaming from the narrow windows, the hall was completely empty.

She strode across the hall, kicking chunks of meat and splattering through puddles of wine, glancing up to meet the stares of the villagers now leaning against the wooden rails of the gallery, where they'd laid pallets for what might be a very long night. She flung the door open to the courtyard, not knowing what to expect.

She splayed her hand against her stomach as if to stop its turning. There her father was, sitting on his restless horse in the middle of the courtyard, sword raised, ordering her great-uncle to raise the portcullis and Sir Rostand to lower the drawbridge while many of his other knights saddled around him. There was her father, shouting in red-faced fury that once St. Simon was found, he'd put his head on a spike for the Prince of Wales to see.

Her brother came up beside her with the sound of his dragging foot. "Is he leading a search party for the prisoner?"

"Yes."

"Father shouldn't leave," Laurent said. "He's taking too many men out of the castle."

"I know."

"We need those men here," Laurent insisted. "In case the prince and his army come."

From her perch at the top of the stairs, she swept the ramparts with her gaze to assess how many men-at-arms her father had left behind to defend the castle. Her heart dropped as she finished the count too quickly.

Laurent said, "Perhaps the prisoner didn't get far. Perhaps father will return before the English army arrives."

"Of course he will," she said. "Sir Jehan has a limp, he couldn't have gone far." She hoped her voice sounded more confident than she felt. Her father would likely search the hills and the deep woods to the north, where an escaped prisoner could more easily hide, rather than over the open fields to the southwest through which the prince would likely march.

Her father and his men wouldn't even see the danger until the English army poured over the ridge.

"I saw you two," he said, his dark gaze sliding to her. "This morning, in the courtyard, walking around together."

She flushed, remembering the sight of Jehan's broad shoulders descending as he crouched to nuzzle one of the hounds, the bare skin of his neck exposed as he bent his head. Her father intended to aim the sharp edge of a sword at Jehan's vulnerable nape, forever snuffing out the teasing light in the knight's brilliant blue eyes.

She mentally shook the thought out of her head. "While we were walking about, Sir Jehan was probably counting barrels of arrows and the number of knights on the ramparts all the while."

"He wanted to kiss you."

I wanted to be kissed. "Can you read minds now, *frai?*"

"Everyone in the courtyard was chattering about it. I'm not blind, either. Sir Jehan couldn't stop staring at you."

She cast Laurent a glare, noticing the frown on his face as well as the sword strapped around his hips and the dagger in his boot. "Mindless chivalry, Laury, nothing else."

"That might be enough."

"Enough for what?"

"Should Sir Jehan reach the prince's army—"

"Don't speak so," she interrupted. "The prince is miles and miles away and the knight is wounded."

"But should he reach the prince," he persisted, "there's a chance Sir Jehan will persuade Prince Edward not to attack Castelnau."

"Why would he do that? After all the terrible things father has done to him?"

"Because of his tenderness toward you."

The word *tenderness* burrowed deep, spreading

rays of warmth inside her. How much she wanted to hope…but she couldn't let sentiment overpower her good sense.

"This is war, Laurent," she said. "I don't think there's room for tenderness."

CHAPTER EIGHT

Jehan rode over the crest of a ridge and came upon the army of the Prince of Wales.

Four or five hundred men-at-arms were spread out in a field, suited, armed, and mounted, as well as a lesser grouping of rag-tag foot soldiers and a cadre of archers in formation. At their head, the Prince of Wales sat high on his cloth-draped warhorse, the pale gray light glinting off the gold thread of the rampant lions and the fleur-de-lys embroidered upon his surcoat. His polished helmet gleamed in his lap, and the mist caught in his drooping black mustache.

Jehan raised a hand in greeting, rode down the ridge, and pulled his stolen horse to a halt. "My lord."

"By God, St. Simon," the prince barked. "Is that a plow horse you're riding?"

"It is."

"And that cloak looks full of fleas."

"Escape," Jehan said ruefully, "was quite an adventure."

"You have more lives than a cat."

Jehan grinned.

"Tonight you can tell me the whole story," the prince said. "But now we have work to do."

"I heard about Seissan." Jehan cast a wary glance over the mounted men, all those helmeted heads, realizing the army had only just halted. "What bastide is next?"

"Answer my questions first." The prince gestured to his squire who pulled a bladder of wine out of a saddle bag to hand to Jehan. "How many fighting men are within the walls of Castelnau?"

Jehan seized the wine as his ribs tightened. He yanked out the cork and drank deep, taking a moment to think. He told himself that the prince couldn't possibly be considering a siege. There were no trebuchets or other heavy war gear in the field. One glance told him that this highly-mobile army was made for swift, destructive raids, to plunder, burn, and move on.

Still, best to deflect any bad idea the prince might be considering.

"Two score or more men, at least," he said, pulling his lips from the mouth of the bladder. "Once the viscount heard about Seissan, he prepared for the worst. They've got full larders and plenty of fresh water."

"Archers?"

"A dozen or more."

The prince barked a reckless laugh. "This will be fine sport."

The wine in Jehan's stomach soured. "Fine sport, my lord?"

"Overrunning the castle." He waved a dismissive hand. "As easy as scaling the walls at the bastide of Seissan—"

"I counsel against it." Jehan's skin prickled as the prince glared. "Whatever your scout reported to you about this castle, I know better. The open field in front of the gate isn't even large enough to hold half your men."

"Being a prisoner has made you soft."

"I see your army and I know the castle." He straightened on his horse. "To attack would be a waste of time and resources."

"Better to tuck our tails and run away from a challenge, then?"

The prince's voice dripped with sarcasm and the words cut Jehan deep. Jehan wanted nothing more than to rain bloody vengeance on the viscount, but three honorable knights and a brave young woman had risked their lives for his sake. He'd made promises to them all.

"Three knights helped me escape," Jehan said.

"So there it is."

"I have an honor debt to them."

"If they live through the day," the Prince said, "they will be rewarded."

His throat tightened. "There is also a woman."

"Is it she who cut off your balls?"

"She saved my life in defiance of her own father."

"A noblewoman?"

"The viscount's daughter."

"Of noble blood, then, if tainted by her father's rebelliousness." The prince bent his head and slipped the helmet over it. "She'll be under my protection nonetheless."

"My lord—"

Through the open visor, the prince's glare cut through Jehan like steel. "The viscount sealed his fate when he murdered your squire, a boy of *my own house* that I put under *your* protection. Now gird your flea-ridden loins and fight like the knight I know you are, for this cause is as much yours as mine."

The prince turned away and raised his clenched fist. A great metallic rustling began as hundreds of men-at-arms gripped the hilts of their swords. The prince shouted *"Forward!"* and the living mass of men and horses shot up the ridge with a thunder of hooves.

Jehan gripped the leather reins of his stolen plow horse as the army flowed past him. All of his screaming thoughts could not stop it from pouring down the slope, and when they passed he was left with only one thought in his mind.

Aliénor.

His heart pounding, he wheeled his horse and

kicked it hard so it lunged ahead. He followed the line of mounted men surging over the top of the ridge where he could see the limestone walls of the castle tinged pink by the lowering sun. He was too far away to make out those watching from the crenelated ramparts, but some instinct told him Aliénor stood among them, witnessing the approaching danger.

A cold determination stole over him, stiffening his muscles and his resolve.

He *would* protect her.

Beneath him, his stolen mount faltered, slick with sweat. Foam splattered from its mouth. Men-at-arms on fresh horses surged past them, eating up the distance to the bridge across the Arrats River. Around him rose the clatter of armor, the beat of pounding hooves, and a growing cacophony of battle cries as he fell back among the foot-soldiers who trotted by with their scaling-ladders.

With rising dread, he saw the prince's vanguard charge across the bridge. By the time Jehan reached the river, the foot soldiers carrying ladders had shot by him and were now running up the slope toward the castle. He dug his heels into his mount but his horse halted, refusing to go past the village where no doubt the beast had a fine berth in a warm stable. Jehan's hand ached, his head throbbed, and his leg burned like lightning, but he dismounted and abandoned the horse to find its own way home. Then Jehan set off for the cliff path on foot, running in spite of the sear of his leg wound.

Heaving with exertion, Jehan reached the top of the hill. Across the field, he saw a dozen ladders already laid against the castle walls, their bases solid in the packed dirt of the filled-in moat. Men swarmed up those ladders, shields over their heads protecting them against arrows and projectiles hurled from the ramparts. The prince's archers hid behind the pines close to the northwest wall, stepping out to shoot at the viscount's men on the ramparts.

Jehan had seen the prince use these tactics before, overwhelming walled villages and small castles with a shockingly swift, forward rush of mounted troops, but he'd expected Castelnau to put up a better defense than what he was witnessing. Already shouts and grunts and cries came from the ramparts as the Prince's soldiers swarmed over.

Gears ground as the drawbridge dipped, stopped, and then descended again. He heard the loosening rattle of the chains supporting the portcullis. The prince's mounted knights milled on the far edge of the clearing, shields raised against a spattering of arrows, poised for when the drawbridge hit the ground. Jehan saw the prince's squire separate from the mounted knights to gallop in Jehan's direction. The boy handed him a helmet, a baldric, and a sword before riding back to his liege lord.

Jehan set the helmet aside but buckled on everything else as he watched the drawbridge descend.

Hide, Aliénor. For the love of God, hide.

The drawbridge slammed against the ground to reveal a gaping opening into the courtyard, the portcullis already raised. Jehan took off at a limping trot, feeling the tug of his wound as he joined the surge into the castle. The clashing of swords rang throughout the courtyard. Some of the viscount's fighters lay scattered on the ground, wounded, or stood with their backs against the walls with their arms raised, already taken prisoner. He caught a glimpse of Sir Thibaud snarling at an English man-at-arms. He saw Sir Rostand lower his own sword as an English knight pressed steel against his throat.

Then Jehan heard the wail of a hound. His heart thundered. He ran in the direction of the noise and saw Aliénor struggling in a knight's grip.

***

Aliénor shrieked as the knight squeezed her tight. Her cry brought the hounds from all corners of the courtyard.

The knight stopped his pawing and shifted her body in front of him. He pulled his sword and swiped at the hounds. One hound's growl dissolved into a yelp of pain that only enraged the other dogs more. They barked and snarled, blurs of raised hackles, their teeth bared with saliva dripping from their gums as she'd only seen them in the hunt. They backed the knight up against the limestone wall of the donjon— and her with him, as a shield against snapping teeth.

This wasn't real, of course. She wasn't being handled like a sack of grain by an English knight. She was sleeping, and this was a nightmare, the manifestation of everything she'd feared from the moment her father had chosen to leave this castle ill-guarded. Any moment now it would all dissolve before her and she'd find herself in the warmth of her bed, gasping for breath.

Suddenly the knight released her. She glimpsed his raised hand before her feet left the ground. Her forehead connected with something cold and hard. She felt herself falling before blackness clouded her mind.

Sometime later she woke with her cheek pressed against a paving stone. From a distant place she heard the snarls and yelps of her dogs.

"Can you find no better foe, knight, than these hounds and a woman?"

The commanding voice sounded familiar. Not Hugo, though the pitch was as bass-deep. Not her brother, who lay sprawled upon the stones within her sight, still moaning from the cuff he'd taken from her attacker when she'd been seized by the knight. Perhaps it was Thibaud who'd come to her aid, for he'd enough sense not to run away with her father and half the castle's defenses.

"This woman," her attacker growled from close above her, "is mine."

"This woman," said the voice, "is the daughter of Tournan."

"All the better," snapped her attacker.

"Do you disobey the prince's orders?"

"I heard no such orders."

A sword scraped out of its sheath. She tried to raise her head only to have her view blocked by a mastiff who ventured forward to lick her face. She gripped the dog's fur and hugged him, using the steadiness of his massive body to lift herself to a sitting position. She tried to make sense of the shapes in blurring motion before her.

Jehan.

Sensation flooded through her, a bitter wash of shock and anger and relief. He fought bare-headed, his black hair clinging to his forehead and neck. A baldric hung low about his hips. He swung his sword as if unhampered by half-healed wounds though she saw blood spotting his hose.

Her attacker surged. Jehan uncoiled to release a blow with the flat of his sword to the warrior's hip. The man grunted and backed away, then charged anew.

"Stop!"

The bellowed voice came from high above. All she saw, at first, were the muddy, shaggy hooves of an enormous war horse. The knight upon it yanked off his helmet and tossed it to the ground between the knights with a clatter. Even with her senses clouded, she recognized the quartered arms of England and France on his surcoat.

With an awful turning in her chest, she realized

the Prince of Wales stood in the courtyard of her castle.

"Have my knights grown so bored," the prince shouted, "they fight among themselves amid great bounty?"

"This knight," her attacker shouted, "would steal a prize from me."

"No prize of his," Jehan retorted. "This is Aliénor de Tournan, the viscount's daughter."

She became acutely conscious of the prince's perusal. Fighting off dizziness, she used the wall of the donjon to shimmy herself up to her feet.

"So this is she." The prince ran a hand over his drooping mustache. "Not your usual type, St. Simon."

"She saved my life." Jehan stepped between the prince's horse and where she stood, setting the point of his sword to the ground as he grasped the hilt with both hands. "I am bound to protect her."

"As am I." The prince turned his attention to her attacker. "Stand down, knight."

The man huffed, but after a brooding pause, he bowed to the prince and sheathed his sword.

"As for the rest of you," the prince shouted, turning his warhorse about, "smoke the viscount out of the rat hole in which he hides, show mercy to the men-at-arms who surrender, and raise tents in the field for our well-deserved rest." He tossed the reins of his horse to his waiting squire. "We shall gather in the hall anon. I believe the lord of this place is hosting a feast in our honor."

The milling men laughed and cried *huzzah* before setting off on their tasks. Trembling with shock and despair, Aliénor watched as they spread to every corner, running hands over the horses in the stable, making kissing noises to the women clustered by the kitchens, marching Hugo and the stable boys into a guarded circle by the northwest tower along with the wounded men.

Thibaud had once told her Castelnau had never been taken by frontal assault and had never surrendered by siege. It had to have been a lie, all a lie, because within minutes of the prince's knights appearing before the castle gates, all was lost.

Lost.

Her knees went loose. Her head scraped against the wall behind her. She felt the ground rushing up to meet her.

Then Jehan caught her in his arms.

CHAPTER NINE

Jehan had stolen before. He'd attacked grain carts on the road to Toulouse, pinched hams from smokehouses, shot deer in royal forests, and fished in forbidden rivers. He'd stolen leather coin satchels from wine merchants on their way to Bordeaux. Without those thefts, he and his small band would never have survived the long winters between fighting seasons.

As desperate as he'd been, he'd always set rules so he could sleep easier. He'd never stolen from those poorer than him, never killed for what he'd set his eye on, and never seized more than he'd needed.

But now guilt slid into him like an icy sword. Where he stood in the war-ravaged courtyard, he cradled Aliénor, her head in the crook of his elbow, his other arm around her back. He watched her bloodied face as she fought her way back to consciousness. When she finally did come around, and the fog of pain and confusion cleared, the look of accusation she threw at him dug into his chest like a gambrel hook. It pierced his lungs and forced the breath out of him.

He knew what guilt felt like, but he'd never experienced this gut-deep conviction that he'd done something unforgivable.

He braced for the fury to come. He waited for her to pummel his chest with her fists, scrape fingernails down his cheek, or kick his shins with her booted feet. But she only stared at him, persisting in stillness.

"Aliénor."

Her name left his lips like a plea. She pushed at his arm and he had no choice but to release her until she stood, weaving, on her own two feet. All around them knights shouted orders, dogs whined, horses shook themselves, and men-at-arms scuffled across the paving stones. A wounded man nearby ventured to stand up, breathing hard as he braced one hand against the donjon wall.

"I tried," Jehan said, curling his hands into fists. "I tried to stop all this."

Words crowded his throat, excuses and explanations, but her face screamed disbelief. She had no way of knowing how much worse this attack could have been, if the prince had set his knights loose to plunder, burn, riot and rape. Instead, the prince had commanded everything set to order. From the look

Edward had given him, Jehan knew it had been a concession to his wishes alone.

She spoke, slurring her words. "I'm a prisoner."

"No."

"The prince himself said so."

"You're under his protection, and mine. You'll be treated with respect."

"In a tower cell?"

"Of course not." Frustration flooded through him. Once again he was the enemy. "I'll escort you to your room."

"Where I'll be locked in."

"For your own good."

She turned, unsteady, toward the donjon stairs. The dogs followed at her heels, whining and shoving their snouts under her hands. He stepped in front of her to swing open the donjon door, revealing a scene of revelry in the great hall. Raucous laughter filled the room. The knights, having wrestled a barrel of wine upon the table, pulled out the bung and took turns tipping the wine into each other's mouths. Jehan tried to be unobtrusive as he steered her toward the stairs to the gallery, but still the men shouted leering encouragement. Jehan threw them a few rude gestures. An icy fear gripped him at the thought of what might have happened if he hadn't intervened, along with the sinking realization that she would blame him for everything anyway.

At the top of the stairs she walked along the gallery to where a crowd of women peered out a door to the hall below. As they caught sight of Aliénor, they curtseyed and made a path for her to enter.

She turned to the hounds and ordered them to sit, and then she raised her pained brown gaze to his. "You've sworn to protect me, Sir Jehan. Protect my women as well."

"With this sword," he said, grasping the hilt, "and with my body."

"I'll hold you to that promise."

She entered the room and closed the door behind her.

After he heard the snick of the bolt, he leaned against the wall. Straightening his wounded leg, he sank to his haunches with the dogs.

***

Two days later, Jehan was summoned to the upper chamber the prince had claimed as his own. Jehan entered the round tower room to find a squire dressing Edward in armor.

"The search party finally returned," the prince said, raising his arms so the squire could slip a padded doublet over his head. "The viscount is nowhere in these hills."

"A pity."

Edward cast him a frowning glance. "That's it? No determination to see his head on a pike? No sworn oaths of bloody vengeance?"

Jehan breathed in hard. Vengeance had no

attraction while Aliénor still refused to talk or even look at him. "The viscount," he said, "is a damned coward."

"Indeed he is, taking his strongest fighters and leaving his daughter and his vassals unprotected. I would think you'd want to cut off the traitor's balls and serve them to his hounds."

"Better he lives to rage that he has lost everything to you, my lord."

"Now there's my wild woodland knight."

The prince's teeth flashed but Jehan felt no mirth. "Are you heading out on a new chase?"

"No. The traitor is a sparrow, not worthy of the hunt." The Prince bent his head as the squire slipped a chain-mail shirt over his head. "We're marching out of this cold, miserable castle within the hour."

Warnings rang in his head. "Which men will you leave me?"

"Why would I leave you men at all?"

"To hold the castle."

"You're coming with me." Edward shrugged the chain mail down his torso. "This place is nothing more than a hut on a hill."

Jehan had heard similar words when he'd taken over Castétis. Edward had dismissed it as nothing more than a hunting lodge. For a prince of England, even such a place as Castelnau, with its eagle's-eye view of the river valley, wasn't worth the trouble of a second thought.

"My lord," Jehan said, treading carefully, "if you

leave this castle unguarded, the viscount will return and take it back."

"Not likely. Tournan was last seen heading north. Running like a rabbit to his traitor lord, King Jean, no doubt."

Jehan's jaw tightened as thunder grumbled outside.

"As pleasant a diversion as this was," the prince continued, "and as pleased as I was to see you free of that traitor's grasp, I didn't come to Gascony to capture castles. I came to burn a swath from the sea to Carcassonne and teach these treasonous lords who is the true king of France."

Jehan clenched his hands into fists. "You'll burn the village."

"The village as well as what I can of this castle, if this damned rain permits. If the viscount does scuttle back, I want him to return to a place bereft of roof-beams, stables, kitchens, provisions—"

"Then you'll leave a formidable enemy at your back."

"Come now. We swept over these walls like the sea."

"They were more thinly defended than we knew, and overwhelmed by the size of your army. But if the viscount returns with the Count of Armagnac and his army—"

"You are overly concerned, Sir Jehan." Edward hiked his hands on his hips as his squire laced up the chain mail. "I wonder why."

With wariness, Jehan met the prince's knowing gaze. He had always suspected that Edward took so quickly to him because they'd caroused together, fought together, and whored together all while coming of age. The other reason was revealed during a long, drunken night, when the prince had admitted how much he admired men who had built reputations from nothing but brawn, bravery, and determination. Undiluted merit, he'd called it, unsullied by the advantages that royalty bestowed.

Jehan supposed it was inevitable that the prince would know there was something more than chivalry involved in this matter.

"Twenty men," Jehan insisted, "and I will hold it all, a bulwark of supplies in the middle of enemy territory."

"I don't need a bulwark of supplies. What I need is one of my fiercest, most fearless knights beside me."

"A foot soldier can burn a village as well as anyone."

"If Armagnac comes out of hiding, it will be knights I'll need. And think of the pillaging in Carcassonne. Would you give it all up for a good tumble?"

His mind screamed *I will not dishonor her* even as his skin went hot with the thought of her naked body.

"God's Blood, you should see your face." The prince frowned and ran his hand over his mustache. "This pretty blond has dug her talons deep."

"I could not call myself an honorable man," Jehan said, "if I didn't protect a woman who risked so much for my safety."

"And what of the bounty I offered you last night?"

Jehan breathed hard through his nose. He had wondered if the prince would bring up his offer again, or if it had only been something mentioned in a moment of drunken generosity.

"Speak, man!" The prince leaned toward him. "Did the Gascon wine make you deaf? Am I throwing English pearls before swine?"

"I heard your promise, my lord." In the past, the prince had made plenty of assurances of great riches to him, but none as solid and immutable as what he'd offered this time. "It's burned into my mind."

"I have favored you in this, Jehan. I planned it as a surprise long before I arrived. Don't make me regret my generosity."

Jehan bowed, playing the humble knight. "You grant me much honor." He straightened up. "Now let me prove I deserve it."

For Aliénor's sake.

"Damn it." Edward huffed his impatience as he shrugged into his surcoat, quartered with the arms of England and France. "Oh, very well. I'll leave you ten of the lightly wounded to guard the ramparts for now. The more seriously wounded will stay as well, but—" he barked, his voice echoing off the rafters "—only until they're healed enough to take over defense.

Then you must send the first group forward to meet me and let the others take their place."

He hoped his expression didn't reveal too baldly his rush of triumph. "I will hold this castle well, my lord."

"I'm sure you'll hold *her* well." The prince seized his baldric from his squire's hands. "And when you're done enjoying this little affair, Jehan, make allowances for the lady's upkeep and then return to your duty. We winter in Bordeaux."

***

"Are they truly gone, my lady?"

"It appears so."

Perusing the scene outside the arrow-slit window, Aliénor squeezed Margot's hand. Behind her in the room, the village woman hovered, ignoring the racing and jumping of children who'd been kept too long cooped up in a single place. They'd all spent the morning listening to the pounding of footsteps, the snorting of horses, and the bantering of men, fearing in the activity some new mischief.

Now the area in front of the castle was punctured with holes from tent-spikes, spotted with flattened grass, and edged with the smoldering remains of cook fires. That and the muddy churn of horses' hooves were all that remained as evidence the Prince of Wales' army had spent days camped in and around her castle.

A sharp knock on the door made her heart jump. She knew who it was, though she could not say why.

She ran a hand down her blue kirtle until she felt the cold links of her belt under her palm. She resisted the urge to gather up the links even though her hands itched to grip something solid. So much of what had happened felt unreal, nightmarish, and she wasn't so confident about what was to come, either.

Nonetheless, she took a position in the middle of the room and faced the door. "Margot, invite him in."

Her maidservant opened the door. Sir Jehan stood before it, his fist raised for another knock. He was dressed in chain mail with a sword at his hip, his surcoat bearing English colors, reminding her that she had every reason to despise him. She dropped her gaze and sucked in a breath. What was done was done. Her father used to rage against every injustice—petty or not—and that had often led him to folly. The future was what mattered now, and her desperate hope for a place in it.

"How do you fare, my lady?"

His voice was pitched low and soft. "Well enough," she said, ignoring how her brow still throbbed where she'd struck the wall. "I see the prince's army is gone."

"Yes."

He stepped inside her bedchamber, his boots soft in the rushes. A little frisson trembled through her. He was her father's prisoner once, abused and neglected, with plenty of reason for vengeance. He'd played the troubadour while strolling around the courtyard, speaking to her in dulcet tones, claiming he wanted her good favor. But she did not really know this man who'd led the Prince of Wales over the ramparts of her castle, no matter what her heart whispered.

"I came to tell you," he said, as the toes of his leather boots came within sight of her lowered gaze, "that the prince has left me in charge of this castle. He also left men-at-arms to guard the ramparts."

"He'll return?"

"Perhaps. But not for some time."

"So you're the master of Castelnau."

"For now."

"I congratulate you, Sir Jehan. Is the prince burning the village as we speak?"

He didn't respond right away. Perhaps she'd spoken the words with more acid than she intended.

"Fortunately," he said wryly, "it's been raining for days. There'll be no burning."

She heard gasps of relief from the women in the room. She knew she should thank Jehan, but she couldn't quite summon the words because he was the one who had brought the devil to her castle in the first place.

But she *did* dare a glance at him. She noticed that he'd taken some care in his appearance. His jaw was clean-shaven, his hair still damp from a wash. It was swept off his face so that she could see the tracks of his comb in the thick, crisp waves. His broad, muscled shoulders stretched the surcoat tight.

This was no longer the weak, suffering, bloody knight she'd tended to in the dimness of the cell in the northwest tower, indeed.

Calm yourself. Forget who he was, remember who he now is. Seize the opportunity you've been waiting for.

"I suppose, Sir Jehan," she said, drawing herself up despite the twinge in her still-sore ribs, "that the castle needs to be put in order and the wounded need tending."

"Yes," he said, with an edge of surprise. "That's why I'm here."

"The villagers can return to their homes, I presume?"

"Of course." His lashes flickered as if he'd just become aware of the listening crowd. "Report back with any needed repairs and we'll see them done before the worst of winter."

She said, "Is the cellar emptied of provisions?"

"Not emptied."

Her jaw tightened at the equivocal answer. Winter yawned before them, the fields were stripped of the harvest, and everything the villagers had stowed away had likely been stolen by the prince's men. Another difficult winter stretched ahead, but she could not let the women and children feel a breath of her worry.

"I'll see to the household," she said, "and put everything in proper order. Are you to set a guard on me?"

"Aliénor—"

"Mademoiselle will do."

His clear blue gaze lay upon her with a curious intensity. "You are free," he said, as a muscle moved in his jaw, "to wander the castle and keep."

"That will make my task easier."

To find her brother, at least, whom she had last seen struggling to his feet in the courtyard. Laurent hadn't visited her in the last few days, so she could only assume he'd been hiding. It was always prudent to avoid being identified as a male heir of the blood when one's own castle was conquered by an enemy.

"Sir Thibaud is asking for you," Jehan said.

Her heart fluttered. "You know that he's a Pirou, not a Tournan. My late mother's uncle, not a blood relative of my father."

"As I am aware." His voice as dry as an old bone.

"Is he well?"

"He suffered a leg-wound, but he's all the prouder because of the scar it will give him, one among many."

She blinked, nonplussed, for that sounded just like her uncle. "Did you throw him in a tower cell?"

"He's in the hall, nursing a cup of wine." His voice darkened with annoyance. "He's being treated with the respect he is due as a knight, as are all the men-at-arms."

She headed to the door. "I'll tend to him first."

He gripped her arm as she passed. Her heart leapt. She was acutely aware of his height, of the luster and thickness of his chestnut-black hair, of the great width of his shoulders. She smelled the freshness of rain on his tunic. She heard the slight scrape of his armor plates as they moved against one another. Her heart beat erratically and she wondered why the room suddenly seemed so hot.

"We must talk," he said.

She could hardly muster the breath to speak. "Some things are best left unsaid."

"I will have my say, and I'd prefer it when we don't have so avid an audience."

Aware of the regard of the crowd upon them, she held her tongue and simply nodded. He loosened his grip and let her go.

She didn't breathe freely again until she was halfway to the great hall, running her palm against the gritty wall to prevent herself from tumbling headlong down the stairs.

As far as she could discern, there was only one thing she and Jehan had any reason to discuss in private.

Hope made her blood rush, but hope was a fragile and dangerous thing.

In her battered heart, she had only one hope left.

CHAPTER TEN

The knock on Jehan's bedchamber door was quick and sharp, as was his reaction when the door swung open.

He paused unlacing his doublet. "Aliénor."

She dipped her head, but his surprise only deepened. She'd long had the servants clean up the remnants of dinner and then ordered the lingering knights to find their pallets. Now moonlight poured through the arrow-slit window of his room, falling in hazy rays across the space between them, and the only ones likely awake in the whole of the castle were the two of them.

He sucked in a deep, steady breath.

"You said earlier," she said hardly above a whisper, "we should talk."

Indeed he had. But he'd imagined it would be the two of them at the trestle table, with all others out of earshot and a flagon of wine between them. That intention had been thwarted when she'd spent the day striding around the place, ordering the dirty rushes to be swept, new ones laid down, an inventory of the provisions to be taken, the wounded to be tended to, and dinner served, all with a reassuring efficiency.

A rustling in the corner reminded him they weren't the only ones awake. Esquival, a new squire who'd been assigned to him by the prince, shuffled up from his pallet to stare, mouth agape, at the woman who'd arrived.

"You," he said, redirecting the boy's gaze. "Outside. Stay by the door."

Aliénor waited until the door closed behind the boy before lifting a brow and saying, "Keeping him close," she said, "in case I decide to murder you in the throes of my despair?"

Her tone was light despite her words. He tried to better read her expression in the flickering shadows, but since the English army had poured over the ramparts and turned them into enemies again, she'd been a stone-faced mystery.

He said, "I'd have kept him inside the room, mademoiselle, if I thought murder was your plan."

"You know very well I can't overpower you, Sir Jehan."

"A well-placed dagger can fell the largest of men."

"I spent the day tending to wounds." She passed her hand through the air. "Such bloody sport, I'm done with it."

"Poison, then?" he prodded, hoping to fan the faint spark of playfulness. "Is that your weapon of choice?"

"Now there's a thought." She tilted her head. "I *do* have access to the food."

He ran his hand over his jaw with a mock frown. "Perhaps I should choose someone to taste my dinner from now on."

"Whether you need to," she said, "depends upon what you have to say to me tonight."

"Then I'd best start with the most favorable news, shouldn't I?"

She gifted him a smile. "I would like to know what your plans are for my future, if you've made any."

Always level-headed, always practical, was Aliénor de Tournan. "I won't send you to a convent," he said. "I promise you that."

Surprise and relief flashed across her pale face. "Well," she said on a rush of breath. "Another reprieve."

"It'd be like winding a funeral shroud around a young filly."

"And there you go, playing the troubadour again."

"I tried to stop all this, Aliénor."

She raised a hand, shaking her head.

"The prince was waiting beyond the ridge, his men in formation." He'd practiced these words a dozen times in his head. "Whether I had escaped or not, the prince intended to attack and nothing I would have done or said could have changed that."

"Please, Sir Jehan—"

"It was all part of a larger plan. Burn Gascony from Seissan to Navarre to Carcassonne. When I showed up, the prince only became more determined—"

"Stop." Her pale palm gleamed by the light of the moon. "Not so long ago, you and I promised to avoid certain subjects."

He grunted an assent. "Your father."

"And Castétis."

"I remember."

He had flirted with her in the sunlight, and then she'd looked at him for a long time, lips parted, heavy-lidded.

She said, "Let's add your liege lord to the list. At least for now."

"Done." He would have agreed to anything just for the remotest chance that she'd look at him with trust.

"So," she said softly, "were there any other plans you wanted to tell me about?"

She placed the candle on the seat of a three-legged stool, then straightened and clasped her hands together, tilting her face in expectancy.

Suddenly he found himself adrift. He'd been determined to speak his case, to help her grapple with the new reality that left her without position or dowry or property except what lay in the bride's chest in her room. Certainly, he had more to tell her. A hundred thousand things. But right now he could think of nothing but how fetching she looked, standing in his bedchamber bathed in moonlight.

"Sir Jehan," she said, seizing the tippet of her sleeve and weaving the tapering fur between her fingers, "is there nothing more you wish to say to me?"

"I have too much to say."

And, since yesterday, no right to speak.

"Then perhaps you'll allow me to make a request."

"Anything."

Her cheeks rounded under the pressure of a smile. "You would do better to hear what it is first."

He didn't care what it was, so long as it kept her smiling for a little longer.

"Before I ask," she said, "there's something I must know. Are you now the Viscount of Tournan?"

He raised a brow. "Is this not on the list of forbidden subjects?"

"Not precisely."

He frowned, considering his words. "Your father lives, so he holds the title, still. The prince may someday decree it belongs to me because we hold possession of the castle and the lands. But the truth is the title will be in dispute until this conflict between the kings is settled."

"It's complicated, then."

"As all things in war."

"Then I ask you this: Are you a good man?"

For the life of him, he could not follow the twists and turns of her thinking. "I'm better than some," he said, fragments of his life as a sell-sword flashing through his mind. "Worse than others. A man is hardly a fair judge of his own character."

"Would you treat a man fairly, and with kindness, although you may think he's a threat to you?"

"A man?"

"Yes."

A dark thought slithered through his mind. "Is there a man in this castle who threatens me?"

"He doesn't," she said. "But you may perceive him thus."

"Speak plainly, Aliénor."

She sighed, swept the candle off the three-legged stool, and sat in its place. "I have a brother."

"Yes." Sir Rostand had told him about the boy when he'd confessed Aliénor was the new heir. "He's got a bad leg."

"Yes" Her shoulders rose as she took a deep breath. "He's here."

"Here?" He stiffened. "In this castle?"

"He's harmless," she said, setting the candle on the floor, safely away from the drag of her tippet sleeves. "He wants nothing more than to be sent to a monastery—"

"The prince was told he *was* in a monastery." His jaw tightened. "By every man-at-arms, every servant—"

"On my orders."

He huffed an angry breath. "God's Blood, woman, where's he hiding?"

"In a safe place." She clutched her hands in her lap and glanced at him from beneath her lashes. "He's had a lot of practice hiding from men who mean him harm."

"And you think I would murder him, as your father murdered my squire?"

Her throat flexed as she seized one tippet and began to come her fingertips through the fur.

"Answer me."

"I think you're the greatest danger he's ever faced. And I don't trust my *own* judgment about you."

She shot up from the stool and turned away from him, pivoting so swiftly that he could not see her face. She paced, running her hands over her flat belly as if to calm some tumult within.

"Your brother will no longer hide in corners like a frightened hound," he said, crossing his arms. "He will sleep in his own bed. He will take his place at table."

Her pacing paused.

"I will do him no harm, Aliénor."

"You promise?"

"Yes."

Then, somehow, he found himself standing in front of her, clutching her elbows. He needed her to trust him. His fingers traced the lacing on the underside of her sleeves as relief softened the lines of her face.

"He's not even the true heir," she said, her voice husky. "My brother, I mean."

He nodded but his attention was diverted. The candle flickering by the stool cast the ends of her hair in fiery gold.

"Laurent was happy to be dispossessed. He brought it about himself."

Her words were like dust motes, cartwheeling out of his focus in favor of the shadow formed in the hollow behind her collarbone.

"That's why *I* am my father's heir." She met his gaze, her brown eyes pleading. "Which makes things so simple for us, don't you think?"

He barely heard her. He caught the word *simple.* It should be a simple thing not to kiss her. He'd stolen so much from her already. He should not steal this, too.

He wouldn't touch her.

He wouldn't kiss her.

He heard the sibilant vibrations of a muffled gasp as he pressed his lips upon hers. All the world narrowed down to the taste of her kiss, heat and moisture and new wine, and the feel of her soft mouth pillowing beneath his. Her smooth cheek filled his palm. The small muscles of her face moved in his cupped grip as she tilted her head for him. Her lashes brushed his cheek as he drew her plump lower lip into his mouth. He released her lip slowly, savoring the taste of her with a groan of hunger that had nothing to do with food and everything to do with a need to kiss every inch of her.

A fraction of his better nature held him back, waiting for her to rescue him by resisting his kiss or murmuring in maidenly modesty or pushing him away—she should, she would, she *must*—but when she parted her lips at the first venture of his tongue and then grasped the edge of his doublet, all his fevered imaginings returned to him in a blast that burned away the last of his better sense.

He sank his hand into the supine give of her lower back. His imagination tumbled forward and then the whole world tilted. He heard a scuffle of footsteps and realized they were his own as he urged her across the room to his bed.

The realization returned a small portion of his sanity. He drew away from her mouth and buried his face in her hair, trying to do what was right while breathing in the green-field scent of new-cut clover in her hair.

His heart was still pounding in his ears when she leaned away from his chest so she could look into his face.

"I'd hoped this was why you wanted to talk to me alone," she whispered.

Her dawning smile stole from him the power of speech.

"It's the only solution, isn't it?" A soft laugh slipped from her lips. "The castle, the lands, and the title of Viscount of Tournan will be yours without question, once we're married."

***

Aliénor watched as Jehan's face stiffened to stone.

And for a stunned, strange moment, all she could think of was how, when she was young, when the castle swarmed with more people than now, she used to chase her brothers up to the ramparts as the broiling heat of the summer triggered violent thunderstorms. She and Bertrand and Gaston would race back and forth, opening their mouths to the sky, crying out as thunder shuddered through the stones. She had adored the noise and the roar and the soaking, and mourned when it all ended, left with nothing but the ghost of forked lightning against the inside of her eyelids.

Hope was like that. It roared and crackled and filled her with excitement before it crashed and burned to ashes.

She drew away from the ghost of her own hope reflected in Jehan's eyes. Her feet scraped against the dried rushes as she buried her emotions in some back chamber of her heart.

How could she have been so wrong? He said he would not send her to a convent. He'd given Thibaud full access to the castle without restriction. And he'd promised to treat Laurent with the same respect.

And he'd *kissed* her until her heart had beaten so hard it had felt as if it were trying to beat its way out of her chest.

She pressed a hand against her swollen, tender lips, not from pain but from all-too-sweet memory. A numbness seeped through her body. Her experience with men was thin, admittedly, but hadn't she heard enough kitchen-talk to know that all kisses didn't feel like this? For most men, she'd been told, kissing was a matter of slobbering and pawing. Then she remembered Jehan had pulled away—though she'd been tugging on the doublet laces to remove what was left of his clothing.

Yet now he stood as still before her as a statue in some bishopric church.

She turned her back to him. It had been all but impossible to keep her mind on their conversation before, when he stood before her with his doublet open, showing the hard planes of his chest. She could not bear to look at him so undone now, while shame crept over her, when all hope for an honorable future was lost.

"Aliénor…"

A scraping in the rushes alerted her to his approach behind her. She tensed as he lifted her hair from her shoulders. By the gentle tugs she felt against her scalp, she knew he was combing it with his fingers. Subtle waves of pleasure flowed through her and she had to fight the urge to let her eyes flutter closed.

"In all my years in the prince's court," he said, "among the prince's courtiers, their sisters, their daughters, and their educated wives, I have never met a woman quite like you, Aliénor."

She stared blindly into the moonlight coming in through the arrow-slit window, warning herself against soaking up his words.

"Even in the cell, when I was beaten and bloody and full of vengeance, you looked me straight in the eye. And when I found you in the courtyard, after the army overran this castle, you were fighting against a knight, determined to stand your ground though he was twice your size."

Foolish courage, she thought. Fruitless defiance was her only bulwark against a fate over which she had no control.

"Everything you do, everything you say," he continued, "encourages me to tell you the truth, as harsh as it may be, so you can face it, conquer it. Your courage makes it very hard for me to save you from…"

False hopes.

She swallowed hard.

"How am I supposed to protect you, Aliénor?" He worked her hair while the tension drained from her neck. "These past days I have fought a battle I cannot win. I am your enemy and yet I want to be worthy of you. I want to win your heart, but, as of yesterday…I no longer have the right to try."

He was trying to tell her something, but his voice

was a low, rumbling hum drawing her body out of the numb shock cocooning her, making every bone and sinew alive to his presence, making her wish he would stop talking and kiss her again.

"Were the world different," he said, "I would make you my wife."

Her breath shuddered out of her, and the sensations that coursed through her made her realize how much she'd wanted to be his woman, above and beyond the position and security that it would give her.

"Were my fate within my hands, I would speak vows in a chapel before every vassal, every villager, every man-at-arms here, promising to take you as my own—"

"Jehan, please," she whispered, "don't ply me with pretty words if—"

"It's my heart that speaks."

She swayed back, or perhaps he stepped forward, but suddenly she felt his face against her hair.

"Though my heart belongs to you," he said, his voice muffled, "my right to marry belongs to the prince."

She hardly heard the last part of his sentence. His words *my heart belongs to you* were like starbursts in her mind. She willed him not to speak any more, for if he continued, then she would know exactly why he couldn't marry her and this moment would end. She'd never yearned for love—she knew it existed for some, the lucky ones, those who could choose their spouses—the village girls and their ruddy-cheeked swains, doe-eyed in the chapel. But for a woman of property, for her, the best she could hope for was the kind of warm affection that blossomed over years between two people who'd been married to raise a family. If they were kind to one another. If they were lucky.

"You need to understand that the prince arranged it while he was in England," he said gravely. "There's a contract with an English widow. Soon to be my betrothed."

Betrothed.

Her heart stopped. Her throat constricted to the point where she could hardly breathe. He was promised to another woman. Promised by the Prince of Wales, someday to be King of England. What a fool she was to not have considered this, that his liege lord would bind him with castles and lands. The truth rose up before her like a thick curtain wall that could never be breached. Not by one woman, a poor woman, a prisoner in her own home.

"I shouldn't have kissed you," he murmured into her hair. "I did not mean to make you think—"

"If you won't send me to a convent," she interrupted, summoning up what little pride she had left, "and you can't make me your wife, then what would you have me be?"

"You'll be the keeper of this castle."

"Chatelaine," she said.

"Yes."

"I already am chatelaine."

"A fine one, turning around an army-scourged fortress within a day—"

"My father made me chatelaine," she interrupted. "He kept me here, little more than a servant, while he marched off to war, while my prospects grew ever fewer with the years."

Until now, when there were no prospects at all. She'd thought this through in the days she stayed in her room until she could think about it no longer. Would her father come and rescue her, with an army behind him, to seize this castle back? Only if King Jean would give him men. How was he to do that, with rumors of war fomenting? It could be another year, two, depending on the needs of King Jean and the whims of war. And why would her father even *bother* to come back? He'd just spent two years in Italy, fighting for a Florentine lord, because he knew better how to make war than to live in his home castle in peace. She could be forever waiting for him to settle her into a better life. Waiting, as a servant in another man's home, perhaps serving another man's wife.

Would her fate forever lie in other men's hands?

She looked at her trembling fingers and saw them covered with the white fur combed from the tippet of her surcoat.

She filled her lungs deeply, fighting off a looming desolation, a growing despair. All she wanted was her family to be safe. For Laurent to be safe, for Thibaud to be safe. And maybe, for her, a small taste of what it meant to be truly happy.

She closed her eyes tightly. His fingers were still tangled in her hair. He pulled them free, and then he slipped his arms around her. He held her loosely but with care, so that she could pull away whenever she wanted, giving her the freedom of her own will.

But she didn't want to pull free of Jehan. Encircled by his embrace, a warmth and calm came over her, a sense of peace that cleared the tumult in her head. An idea came to her, as clear and bright as stars on a winter night. The solution to all her problems was not in her hands, but she saw a slim and narrow path to happiness..

She leaned back a fraction so the beating of his heart vibrated against her back, and dared to speak her heart. "I think there may still a place for me here, Jehan."

"I have promised." There was a strain in his voice, a stillness in his limbs. "You'll be my chatelaine."

She ran a hand up his warm, muscled arm. "I'll be your mistress as well."

CHAPTER ELEVEN

A swooping sensation weighed in his loins as fast as her words registered. Her backside brushed against him as she turned in his arms to face him with determination and intent in her eyes.

God's Blood.

His will stretched as thin as the linen separating his flesh from hers.

He'd be a liar if he said he didn't want this.

Hadn't considered every possibility of it while sleeping outside her door with the hounds.

Hadn't examined all possible consequences.

Hadn't dreamed about it, every damn night.

She slid her hands under the cloth of his doublet to press her palms against his chest. His heart threatened to thunder out of his skin.

He caught one of those hands in his. "You don't mean this."

The moonlight, falling from behind her, lit the curve of her cheek as she smiled.

"When I said you would be my chatelaine," he added, "I didn't mean—"

"I know your offer is honest, Jehan."

"Take the offer then. As it is."

"I want more."

Her body pressed against his, her hips surging closer to where he most ached, and it took a moment for him to realize that she hadn't moved. It was he who'd released her hand so he could pull her close.

"I have waited too long upon the whims of my father." She feathered her fingers up the side of his neck. "I will take matters in my own hands."

A cloud passed across the moon, casting a shadow over them. "Aliénor," he whispered, "I'll be married to another."

"Your English widow won't want to visit a little castle in Gascony." She arched her back under the touch of his fingers. "Surely she'll keep to her grand English manor houses."

His control frayed thin.

"Jehan," she sighed, slipping a finger across his lips. "If you finally had a future within your grasp, wouldn't you seize it with both hands?"

***

Aliénor drew his head lower so she could capture his mouth. He groaned in a way that made his whole body tremble. He tightened his grip around her until her toes rose from the floor. She felt weightless, buffeted, gripped by pleasure. Surely this must be how her hawk felt, set free of the leash, spreading her wings wide and vaulting toward the sky.

He whispered her name. She caught it with the eager press of her mouth. When she turned aside a fraction to catch her breath, his lips slipped up her cheek toward her temple, making her skin tingle. She arched her back in response to the muffled pressure of his roving hand, wishing all the while that they both were naked.

With a rush of awareness she realized she could make it so.

She pressed away from him until a space opened between their bodies. She slipped her hands under the cloth of his doublet and spread the edges apart. Moonlight gleamed on him, all lean planes and shallow, carved hollows, warm and smooth against her fingers.

Warm and smooth against her lips.

His pulse jumped against her mouth and pleasure surged through her. She rasped her thumb across his flat, dark nipple. His gasp made the muscles between her legs tighten.

She hardly knew what she was doing, but she didn't care. She'd waited too long to know what it felt like to fall into a man's arms, feel his breath on her face, feed the hunger growing inside her.

She made short work of the lacings of his

doublet then pushed it off his shoulders. With a swing of an arm he tossed it to some far wall. Then he crossed his arms and seized his shirt in his hands, sweeping it over his head in one swift motion. He wrapped it into a loose ball and sent it off to join his doublet in the rushes.

His small clothes hung low on his narrow hips, revealing a trail of dark hair that started beneath his navel and ended somewhere beneath the linen. She traced the indentation that cut from his hip toward his loins, fascinated by the flex of a muscle beneath her fingertip. Below, his member swelled, tenting the cloth. She let her fingers trail lower to explore. He pulsed hot against her hand.

Breathing hard, she met his gaze. The silver-blue intensity of his look proved he liked what she was doing. Yet he stood patient, his body thrumming-tense but his hands loose at his sides, his chest heaving as he let her touch him.

She tugged the sagging belt loose, and then pulled the waist wide so his small clothes could slide over his member and fall to the rushes. Fully naked, he stood before her, a knight stripped of armor yet intimidating, powerful. The moonlight burnished the muscles that swelled in his arms and legs and rippled down his abdomen.

Her gaze dipped lower. Her insides throbbed as she imagined his thickness pressed into the aching hollow between her thighs.

He grasped her wrist as she reached for him.

"Aliénor," he said, half gasping, "you're trying to kill me."

"No, no," she whispered, but his breathlessness undid her uncertainty. "I just want to touch you."

"And you will." He released her wrist to tug on the neckline of her kirtle. "As I will touch you."

He may as well have showered her with sparks. She reached behind to loosen the laces of her kirtle. She dug her teeth into her lower lip to stop herself from breathing so fast and hard, but her body wasn't completely her own. Her fingers fumbled with the kirtle's back laces, missing loops and tugging the wrong ends.

"I could help," he murmured, with a teasing gleam in his eye.

She breathed an unsteady half-laugh and gave him her back. While he made quick work of the laces, she pulled her neckline loose and went to work on the laces at her wrists. After she'd loosened the sleeves, he slipped his knuckles under the neckline and yanked her kirtle to her feet, where she stepped out so he could sweep it away.

His eyes widened when she turned to him. Her nipples had gone tight under her linen shift, tingling under his gaze. With the moonlight at her back, she knew he could see the whole outline of her body, every curve and shadow.

He likes what he sees.

The thought was like the burn of strong wine. She gathered her shift in her hands, pulling it up so the hem rose above her knees and then her thighs. There, she hesitated, but not for modesty. She paused for something a bit more wicked, something teasing and sly. She was to be his mistress now. A soft laugh came out of her that didn't sound like her at all.

"*Couret.*" The word half warning, half plea.

There was pleasure in the way he looked at her so hungrily. She swept the shift off, leaving her in nothing but her hose, tied with ribbons at the thigh, and her leather slippers.

She gasped as he caught her by the waist, his hands rough against her skin, and lowered himself before her, dragging his head down her body. . His hair brushed against her jaw, her throat, her chest, her breasts, where he made her gasp by sucking a nipple into his hot mouth.

His tongue worked magic and her legs went limp.

"I have dreamed of you like this," he murmured, tightening his grip on her waist.

She couldn't speak as he sucked her nipple into his mouth again.

"I have dreamed of your body against mine," he said. "Your breast against my tongue. Your heart beating hard under my ear."

She ran her hands over his shoulders and down his broad, muscled back, memorizing every swell and flex.

"I will make you happy," he said. "I swear it."

He straightened and lifted her up. She rose dizzy-high in the room as he moved her out of the moonlight. Then he swung her down, lowering her until she felt the softness of pelts against her back.

His hair fell on either side of his face as he hovered over her, staring at her naked body until she flushed.

"Are you to spend the whole night looking," she whispered, "or are you going to kiss me?"

With a groan, he did as she bid. Her breasts brushed against the hardness of his chest. She felt the male part of him, straining against her thigh. He shifted his weight so he could run a hand, flat-palmed, from her shoulder to her breast and over her belly and lower, a sweeping touch that made her shudder with pleasure.

She'd known that there was pleasure in coupling. In a castle as full of nooks and hideaways as this, lovers took what opportunities they could to steal a moment. She'd heard the moaning and the grunting with pangs of gentle envy, and she'd looked forward to when she would enjoy the same with a husband. But she'd always thought the pleasure was purely physical, just a squeezing release of tension like the barn animals in the rutting season, with the males the most pleased by it all. She hadn't expected to want this so much, to crave it in a way that went beyond shivers of anticipation as Jehan's fingers slipped between her thighs.

His breath hissed through his teeth. "You're ready for me."

Jehan found with unerring precision the tight,

aching point of pleasure. He stroked it in tender little circles until she began to make odd little noises of surprise and yearning, the tension inside her growing tighter.

She was half arched off the bed when he paused. She groaned in protest, opening her eyes to find him hovering over her, a vein throbbing in his brow.

He shifted his weight and nudged her thighs wider with his knees. Cold air brushed across her, making her aware of how wet she was, how exposed, how sensitive and aching—and suddenly she remembered that the first time a woman did this, it usually hurt.

She must have stiffened, because he paused and whispered against her cheek. "Tell me again that you want this, Aliénor."

Her heart raced. She wanted this more than anything, even more because it was her own choice.

"Don't stop," she said, "teach me what to do."

His body stiffened. "No regrets?"

"None."

He shifted. The tip of his member slid into her cleft. She clutched his shoulders at the feel of it there. Every thought and feeling focused on how warm and slick and hard he felt, poised there, and how intensely he looked down at her, his jaw tight with control. He seemed to be waiting for something, but she was going to scream if he didn't press deeper. She arched against him, rolling her hips. Then, as he groaned, his mountain of shoulders moved under her hands and he pressed deep into her.

She dug her fingers into his back as her body stretched to accommodate him, bringing a twinging sensation of both pain and pleasure. He pushed in and paused, making a sound to match hers. After waiting a space, he retreated, making her plead not-so-silently for his return. He plunged deeper, but she could tell by the tension through his whole body that he was holding himself back. Shudders rippled through him to match those shuddering through hers.

Soon he stopped pausing between strokes and moved in and out of her with more urgency. His back flexed in marvelous ways beneath her hands. She gave in to an urge to arch her back and spread her thighs wider. He ran his lips along her jaw while he plunged to the root, his breath harsh. Within her, an ache swelled with sudden intensity. Her inner muscles tightened around him. She cried out his name, over and over, while something glorious burst within her, sweeping through her throbbing body.

Moments later, he stiffened, pressing his forehead against hers as a warm wetness bathed her deep inside. She listened to his deep-throated groans with a rush of pure satisfaction. She held onto him as the tension seeped from his body, sinking into a deep comfort as she held him closer, thinking *I love you.*

I love you.

CHAPTER TWELVE

Back when Jehan was a lowly sell-sword, his evenings used to be spent on a horse blanket spread upon the cold ground, dreaming of smoked duck and salted ham, sheep's cheese and roasted chestnuts, a generous bowl of pot soup. As one of the prince's knights, he had swapped cold ground for a hay pallet and an empty belly for a full one, but he still spent evenings dreaming of the new things he craved: Fine swords and new armor. Stables full of horses. Cellars full of wine. Strong-walled castles and the lands to go with them.

Yet, right now, as the black of night lightened to gray and Aliénor still slept beside him, he could think of no greater treasure than the warmth of her in his bed, naked in his arms.

He pressed his nose against her hair and smelled the scent of musk and sunshine and the lingering fragrance of cut clover. She made a little noise and shifted her position under the furs, sliding against his body in ways that warmed his blood.

She murmured, "Is it morning?"

"Not yet, *couret.*" Her low, husky voice set his pulse leaping.

"It's still dark?"

"Shhhh. Sleep."

Defying him, she lifted her head from its burrow. Turning toward the arrow-slit window, she frowned at the hazy cast of a breaking dawn.

"If you keep your eyes closed," he whispered, "it'll still be dark."

"But the servants will be awake soon."

"Let them do their work, then." He kissed her temple, her hair catching on his lips. "Lie abed with me."

Her mouth curved as she rolled into his arms again. "How little you know of managing a castle."

He thumbed a tress off her brow as she blinked open her beautiful dark eyes, his heart pounding to see them heavy-lidded with satisfaction.

"Fires must be lit," she said, trailing a hand over his chest. "Meals must be planned."

"How fortunate I am," he said, "to have such a chatelaine."

A shadow flitted across her face then disappeared, but not before it sliced across his heart like a tip of a dagger.

He couldn't give her what a woman like Aliénor

deserved.

But he knew how to make her happy.

Her lips tasted warm. He ran a hand under the furs, his palm following the curves of her body. She made one of those sweet little noises in her throat that kicked his cock into alertness. Her rosy nipple tightened under his touch. His blood flooded south.

"Tell me," he murmured, sweeping his hand down her belly, "what you like."

"You." She pushed the pelts off in hurried enthusiasm and then reached between them. "This."

On a groan, he lost the ability to breathe.

Startled, she released him. "Did I hurt you?"

"N-no."

"It's so warm." She ventured to touch him again, a teasing run of her fingertips along the ridge. "I can't believe you fit inside me."

He placed a warning hand on her wrist. "Aliénor."

"You promised me."

He couldn't fathom what she was talking about while his cock was gripped in her hot, eager little hand.

"Last night," she reminded him. "You promised I could touch you."

He vaguely remembered he'd said something like that. Gathering what was left of his self-control he released her hand and gave her leave to explore. He tried to temper the blinding rush of his excitement. The shifting pressure of her curious fingers made control difficult.

"It's throbbing," she said, lifting her head off the pillow, all wide-eyed fascination, her skin made pearly by the dawn light.

He could manage nothing but a grunt.

"It's hard but…smooth," she murmured, leaning over him. "And so warm."

Her soft stroking was making him lose the ability to speak, so when she slipped a hand below his cock to explore farther, he grasped her wrist again. "Enough for now."

She narrowed her eyes at him. "You promised–"

"You got your wish, witch."

"It excites you?" She gave him a light squeeze.

"Yes," he said with strain in his voice, "but I want to excite *you* now."

With one swift move, he rolled her flat on her back, her low, husky laughter like music in his ears. He gave her a taste of her own teasing as he dipped his hand between her legs and rubbed his finger across her cleft.

Her laughter ended in a moan. He rose up on an elbow so he could watch her in all her nakedness. Her slim, strong body arched against his touch. Her nipples peaked high and all but begged for kisses. The honey-brown triangle of her woman's hair lay soft against his palm.

She was a wonder. He whispered, "Do you know how beautiful you are to me?"

She didn't answer, only threw out her arms to

grasp the furs tight. The trembling in her body told him how close she was to reaching her pleasure. With one nudge of his knee he stretched her legs apart, eager to slide his aching cock inside her, until he remembered the way she'd flinched last night at the first penetration.

For all her sensual abandon, she had been a virgin to his touch, and sure to be sore this morning. So he pulled his cock away from temptation, slipped down the bedding, and settled between her thighs.

"Don't deny me," she gasped, her fingertips scraping his shoulders. "No more teasing, Jehan—"

She choked on her words as he rubbed his lips over her. She made a surprised noise and went stiff, only to fall back against the pelts when he kissed her more deeply with his tongue. He grasped one breast, massaging gently as the nipple traced circles on his palm. As he tongued the nub of her pleasure, slick with desire, her hips began to roll. She grasped a handful of his hair. He kissed and sucked until she arched and cried out and her wet, tender flesh throbbed against his mouth.

Lost in the taste of her, he released his own pleasure in the linens.

As their breathing filled the room, he dragged himself up to her side. With his arm thrown across his brow, he gazed blindly at the ceiling and yet noticed a thousand little details. The old, dark wood of the roof-beams. The mitering of the stone wall. The scratch of a tip of hay against his back. The warmth of her body and the scent of her sex. The sound of her hair as she turned her head against the pillow. The slip of her small hand into his.

Her brown eyes, soft with a contentedness that made his heart squeeze.

"That," she said, "was different than before."

"You liked it."

She bit her lower lip. He stared, fascinated with the way her lips swelled around the gentle pressure of those lovely teeth.

"I thought it was always the same," she ventured. "Every time."

"There are many ways I can please you."

"But," she said, glancing down his body, "why didn't you…"

"I took my pleasure just watching you."

She curled to her side, one rosy nipple peeking over the bend of her elbow. "Is that possible?"

He nodded. His loins grew heavy just thinking of all he could teach her.

"I didn't think…it would be like this."

His mind vaulted back to swift tumbles in bawdy houses, lusty rolls in the fields, behind haystacks, and in vineyards.

He thought, *It's never been like this before.*

He rolled to his side to face her. "Stay with me today."

"I *am* with you."

"All day. In this bed." It seemed impossible to be aroused so soon, but already his cock swelled. "I'll send Esquival to fetch us food."

His thoughts vaulted forward to what it would be like to feed her with his own hands, to eat off the flat of her belly, to teach her the pleasures of honey, but those thoughts died as her gaze skittered away from his.

"I have duties, Jehan."

She rolled to her feet in one swift movement. He watched the heart-shape of her backside as she strode to where their clothes lay in a tangled heap upon the floor.

"Aliénor," he ventured, sensing a chill that had nothing to do with the weather, "the castle will not fall to pieces if you abdicate your duties for one day."

"But my absence will be noted."

She avoided his gaze as she slipped into her shift. He sat up, swinging his legs over the edge of the bed, and realized that there could be only one reason why she wouldn't want her absence to be noted.

He murmured, "You want to keep this a secret."

Her breasts lifted as she raised her arms to slip into her kirtle. "Is that such a terrible thing?"

"It isn't possible."

"Perhaps not from the servants." She swept her hands over the wool of her kirtle to loosen rushes clinging to the fabric. "It's possible my maidservant has already noticed my absence. Surely Esquival heard us from where he's sleeping just outside that door. I suppose it won't be long before some kitchen maid or man-at-arms notices me coming down from the tower in the early morning."

She yanked upon her sleeve laces, looking everywhere but at him. Fresh guilt speared through him. She'd gone from heiress of the place to mistress of her one-time enemy, all within a few days.

He shouldn't be surprised she'd prefer subterfuge, but it still left him feeling flayed, loathsome.

"I'm not ashamed," she said, as if reading his thoughts. "I have chosen this, and I've done it willingly."

How eagerly he latched onto those words as a salve against guilt.

"I will stand up in the mead hall and take your hand in mine," she continued. "It's just that there are some who will not...approve."

"Thibaud?"

Jehan figured Thibaud *should* disapprove, but the fierce knight struck Jehan as a man of the world. Then he remembered their discussion last night and the truth hit him hard. "Your brother," he said. "It's he who concerns you."

She crossed the space separating them and fell to her knees before him in a heap of skirts. "Laurent will never understand."

"You said he's only a boy."

"He is, but he's so pious and overprotective. He'll spend days petitioning you and praying for my soul."

How could Jehan blame a brother for worrying

about his sister, the woman whose gaze now pled for a solution to an impossible problem? And how long, indeed, could they keep their coupling a secret within a castle full of kitchen gossips and idle, wounded knights?

"It wouldn't be forever," she said, grasping his hand where it lay on his knee. "If we could just hold off the whispers until we send him off to the monastery in Toulouse, then the news will go over easier. Then he won't be here every day, watching us. Brooding."

"I could send a message to the abbot." The prince's army roamed the countryside and French knights gathered to counter-attack, making it a dangerous time for anyone to be on the roads, but a single messenger might avoid trouble.

"If you sent a message today," she said, "then it's possible he'd be on his way in a week or two."

A week or two sounded like an eternity, but he supposed patience was necessary to earn her trust. "I'll send a message. In the meantime, take your brother out of hiding. I would meet this boy you care about so much."

Her face softened in relief.

He added, "Esquival will follow my orders about holding his tongue. Will your maidservant do the same?"

She bobbed her head.

"I warn you, Aliénor." He leaned over to place his hands on her delicate shoulders. "You're still sleeping here."

She cupped his face. "I wouldn't miss a single night."

***

Jehan bounded down the tower steps, feeling more expansive of heart than he had since long before the viscount's attack. He breathed in the life of the donjon around him, noticing the fresh rush lights in the wall sconces, the servants chattering in the rooms he passed as they swept out ashes in the hearths and laid wood for later fires. He paused at the gallery, gripping the railing as he perused the mead hall and the men-at-arms scattered below, honing their swords, cleaning the links of their chain mail, mending their small clothes and hose, and sharing slices of veined cheese and thick, dark bread spread upon the trestle table.

All this was his, and Aliénor, as well, and for a moment—this moment—he stood inside the glamour of his own ambitions.

Then he caught the steady gaze of a certain white-haired knight in the mead hall below. Thibaud had taken to him from the moment Jehan had given him the freedom of the castle keep. The knight had made a point to sit beside him at table and regale him with stories, as if he were trying to make up for the viscount's violence with cordial courtesy. Still, a reflexive kick of guilt drove Jehan to re-examine the events of the morning.

Jehan was sure Aliénor hadn't been seen when she left the upper room. Esquival and presumably Aliénor's maidservant had been sworn to silence. And none of the men in the mead hall were waggling their brows in his direction or giving him a single leering wink. He was imagining things.

Nonetheless, Jehan put more gravity in his stride as he descended to the lower floor. He came upon Aliénor's great-uncle leaning against a wooden gallery-post in deference to his wounded leg.

Thibaud thrust out a cup of wine. "You've lain abed."

"A fine greeting, that."

"Conqueror's prerogative, I suppose."

Jehan seized the cup and took a long sip, hoping Thibaud would assume it was from thirst and not an effort to hide his face while he remembered the conqueror's prerogative he'd spent the night enjoying. When he lowered the cup, he gestured to the clean linen wrapping around the knight's leg. "It pains you still?"

"It's a scratch." Thibaud slapped the wrappings with the back of his hand. "But this wound woke up an older one I received at Crécy."

Crécy, in the north of France where, ten years prior, the English had crippled the French army, giving the English King Edward III his first real victory in this war.

"Yes, Crécy," Thibaud said to his unspoken

question. "I was there. Survived it, obviously."

"Yet all the stories I've heard from you have been about your forays into the Italian states, fighting for Florence with the viscount."

"Is it so hard to believe I fought proudly in King Phillip's personal guard?"

"You've been holding back on me, Thibaud." And not just by conveniently omitting any information about a certain grand-nephew hiding in the chapel. "So you were truly a king's man."

Thibaud shrugged a shoulder. "If I told you, you'd have the prince requesting ransom from the Crown."

"I may still."

"It'd be a fool's errand." The older knight waved a hand. "My king has been dead for nearly five years."

"King Jean has obligations to all his father's knights."

"King Jean saw me beg his father to be released from his service, which he might interpret as nullifying all obligations."

Jehan narrowed his eyes. There must be a reason why Thibaud was telling him all this while blocking his route to the food his belly was rumbling for.

"Are you not curious?" the older knight said. "How I could go from fighting alongside the flower of French chivalry to fighting petty border wars for rich Italians?"

Jehan shrugged. "I know very well how a knight of good name and family can end up selling his sword to the highest bidder."

Thibaud frowned and shook his shaggy white hair. "This is not the same. When your family lost everything a decade ago, you were barely a knight. I lost nothing but pride after Crécy. I could have stayed in the king's service."

The knight was sinking into the tale, but Jehan's belly couldn't wait any longer. He brushed by Thibaud, saying, "Join me at table. Listening to one of your stories requires more than just wine."

Thibaud's hand curled around his arm. "This tale is best told in discretion, Sir Jehan."

"These men-at-arms don't care about—"

"I was not the only one wounded at Crécy." Thibaud lowered his voice. "So was Aliénor's father."

As he spoke her name with that look in his eye, Jehan flinched. Whatever was on Thibaud's mind, now he was sure it had to do with Aliénor.

"You'll want to know this." Thibaud released him and returned to the support of the gallery-pole. "It may explain how you found yourself a prisoner, half-dead in the northwest tower."

Jehan's jaw tightened. "Speak your mind, Thibaud."

"Aliénor's father was found on the battlefield at Crécy bleeding from the head and all but dead. I found him myself."

Jehan crossed his arms, waiting for the knight to get to the point.

"For a while, I thought we'd lost him." Thibaud

squinted off to some far place beyond the walls. "I dreaded telling my niece—Aliénor's mother—of his death, should it happen. They were a love match, the two of them."

The phrase struck him hard. He'd never considered if there even was such a thing, and now it resonated like the pluck of a violin string.

"But he woke up," Thibaud continued, "and over the weeks I saw a different man emerge from the long sleep. He beat his horse when he struggled to climb on the saddle. He pulled a dagger on a man who'd done nothing but give him a sour look. He broke the wrist of a woman who delayed bringing him wine."

Jehan remembered the viscount's contorted face when the madman had killed his squire. The brutal and unrelenting attack had been like a starved wolf falling upon a wounded deer.

"The king as well as Count of Armagnac soon had enough of Guillem and his rages," Thibaud continued. "The viscount was ordered away from court and back to his Gascon holdings, but I couldn't bear to think of him returning in that condition to my unsuspecting niece. So I petitioned the king for leave. Then I bowed to and flattered the damn viscount as if he deserved my sword as protection. I lowered myself to being a mercenary for a man who could only function when he was in the fields, where murder was called war. And I did all this for one reason: To protect my niece and her family."

"And you stayed long after she died," he

ventured, finally seeing the knot at the end of Thibaud's winding yarn, "to protect her daughter."

"As I still do."

The knight nudged the pole with his shoulder to straighten up, his gray eyes so clear that Jehan could no longer pretend Thibaud didn't know exactly what had happened in the upper room of the tower last night.

Between them the knowledge shimmered, the air growing thin.

The old knight said, "You will marry her of course."

His heart squeezed as he lowered the cup. "I am betrothed to someone else."

Thibaud's hand went to his side where the hilt of his sword would have been, if Jehan hadn't disarmed all of the viscount's men. The knight's shoulders tightened and his lips went white, and for a moment Jehan saw him as he must have looked as a king's man, hair flaring wild, ropy muscles flexing, eyes blazing.

Jehan braced himself for a blow from Thibaud's white-knuckled fist. He deserved such a punishment. But Aliénor deserved discretion, and a fight between him and Thibaud would raise questions.

"Challenge me if you will, Sir Thibaud," Jehan said, squaring his stance. "But I won't send away the woman I love."

Surprise and confusion flittered across the knight's face, followed by a deep rippling of his wrinkled brow.

Thibaud said, "So it's love, is it?"

Jehan nodded and held the older man's gray gaze. Thibaud's anger seemed to seep out of him, like wine out of a punctured bladder-skin.

"Life has not treated Aliénor well," Thibaud said, releasing a long, weary sigh. "If you truly love her, then I have to trust that you will."

***

Jehan found Aliénor in the small wooden chapel. She crouched before the altar. The long skirts of her kirtle pooled on the wooden floor, bathed in blue light pouring from the small stained glass window. As he entered and approached, she started to her feet. Only then did he notice the boy in rough weave sitting on the rise to the altar.

She dipped in a curtsey as he approached. "Sir Jehan."

She was as cool as the autumn wind, he thought, but he suppressed a spurt of irritation. This mummer's play was temporary.

He turned his attention to the boy who still sat in a sprawling slump. "So, Aliénor. This is your brother."

"Laurent," she said, turning aside to open up the space between them. "This is Sir Jehan de St. Simon—"

"I know who he is."

Jehan gave the sullen creature a look-over. The boy's black, disheveled hair was blunt-cut, his face dirty, but in a deliberate way, as if he'd smeared his fingers in the ashes. The hilt of a dagger jutted from a rope belt that drew folds of a long tunic against him, making it impossible to see his true size. The boy had the viscount's eyes, as black as midnight, wary and resentful.

"Had I seen you before now," Jehan said, "I'd have known in a moment you were your father's son."

"I *am* my father's son." The boy's voice was a basso timbre, not a crack in it. "And I will hide no more behind pews and altars." He tilted his chin at his sister like a dare. "No, Aliénor, not ever again."

Pushing himself off the altar platform, her brother unfolded to his full height.

Aliénor had been mistaken.

This was no boy.

Jehan slid his gaze to where Aliénor stood, glaring at her brother with nostrils flaring. "Your sister is very protective of you, Laurent."

"And I of her."

"Please, Laurent—"

Ally." The young man pre-empted his sister's retort in a sibling way that brought Jehan a pang of memory. "Do you believe I am as useless as our father thought me to be?"

"Of *course* you're not." She huffed in annoyance. "But already you're acting foolishly overprotective."

"You said I had reason to fear for my life. Are you to kill me, Sir Jehan?" The young man turned to him. "Will you hang me from the ramparts to get rid of any lingering doubt about who owns the land and title?"

"I'll do no such thing."

"So, Ally, who is the overprotective one?"

"It was the prince I feared, but he's gone now. Sir Jehan has an obligation to me. He promises to protect us both."

"I believe my sword," Laurent retorted, "is the only proper protection against the English."

"Stop." Aliénor laid a hand on her brother's arm, but her brother strode away toward the altar rail. The tunic he wore was too long to see his crippled foot, but Jehan heard it drag across the wood in time with his jagged gait.

With a long sigh, Aliénor turned her attention to him. "You see, Sir Jehan, my brother speaks with great passion but little sense."

"Admirably so," he said. "A brother should worry about his sister. You mention a sword," he said, raising his voice to get the young man's attention. "How well can you wield one?"

"Well enough."

"And what if I were to allow you possession of your sword," Jehan added, "as long as you promised not to use it against me or my men, except in sparring?"

"Why would you do such a foolish thing?"

"It's no foolish thing." Jehan strode to the altar rail, shifting a hip upon it to get a better look into this boy-man's face. "If you are half as honorable as your sister, you will be bound by good behavior to keep it sheathed while remaining within the castle walls."

Her brother gave him a look out of the side of his eye, all suspicion and wariness.

Jehan added, "Your sister tells me you want to join the church."

"I'm bound to my family before all."

"She says there's an opening in the monastery in Toulouse."

"You want to get rid of me."

"Laurent!"

"I'm offering you a future," Jehan said, "one I was told you wanted. Have I been as misinformed about this as about"—he glanced over his shoulder and gave her a look with a lift of his brows—"as about certain other things?"

Laurent asked, "But what of my sister?"

Jehan tore his gaze away from her, bathed in blue light, her breasts swelling from the neckline with each breath, worry rolling off her in waves. "What do you wish to know?"

"Is she to go to a convent or to the court of our King Jean?"

"Not to Paris," Jehan said. "The roads are too dangerous for a journey to the French king's court, and will be for the foreseeable future."

"A convent then," her brother said.

Jehan snorted. "I'd have to truss her well to bundle her off to a convent." Was it his imagination, or did he see the boy's lips twitch? "Your sister has agreed to be my chatelaine."

"As I have always been," she said wearily from behind him. "No one knows how to manage these lands better than me."

"The prince shall summon me come the New Year," Jehan added. "I'm to join his army when they return to Bordeaux for the winter. This castle and these lands need keeping. She has offered to do so in my name."

"All the more reason for me to stay," Laurent said. "I won't be like my father, leaving her here with no one to protect her when an army comes pouring over the walls—"

"I will leave enough men to guard the ramparts. Thibaud will be her personal champion."

Her brother found sudden interest in a scratch on the altar rail, tracing it as his brow furrowed. He scraped his bad leg against the floorboards and Jehan could all but see him frowning his way through the options as he struggled between duty and good sense.

"Join me in the mead hall." Jehan slipped off the rail and headed toward the door. "When you're properly dressed and back where you belong, Laurent, you, your sister and I will talk more."

CHAPTER THIRTEEN

Aliénor sat at the end of the trestle table, her nerves as tight as a bowstring. Considering that her world had turned upside down only weeks ago, she should be content with the crackle of the hearth fire and the bounty of food upon the table. Today, Sir Rostand and Laurent had eschewed the cold, drizzly courtyard for the relative warmth of the great hall for his now-daily practice. Between energetic bouts of Laurent's and Rostand's sword play, carried out in a cleared space in front of the trestle table, she could hear soft laughter coming from the servants in the buttery. Pewter plates graced the table and the tapestries had been reattached to the walls as if the prince's attack had never happened.

But this apparent calm felt false, fragile, and ready to snap with one knowing look or ill-placed word.

"You forget that I fought at Crécy, Jehan," Thibaud bellowed, making her start as he banged his fist upon the table. "The English used shameful trickery, putting knights' weapons in the hands of worthless freemen in boiled leather jerkins."

Jehan shrugged. "The Welsh archers are skilled, Thibaud. Their longbows men fire three arrows to a crossbow man's one."

"In my day, no knight of any honor would send the archers ahead of the mounted men, and certainly no king—"

"They would if they knew a Welshman's arrows could pierce a knight's mail." Jehan raised his voice above the fresh crack of wooden swords as her brother and Rostand began another round of sparring. "Try fixing your foot, Laurent. Your bad foot, so you can better maneuver with your better one."

Aliénor watched her brother, grinning and dripping with sweat as he flexed his hand over the hilt of his sword. Amid the clatter and grunts, she couldn't take her eyes off Laurent, obeying Jehan's command with a determined nod.

Wordless obedience, she thought, from a boy who'd once spit fire at Jehan. She should be satisfied that he and Jehan weren't at each other's throats, but she just didn't understand the change of heart.

"King Philip," Thibaud said, waving his cup as wine sloshed over the rim, "now *he* knew how to fight like a true knight. I can't say the same for your liege lord, Sir Jehan—the *bad* foot, Laurent, make a pivot of it."

"Perhaps the French should adapt to changing capabilities."

"By burning villages? Destroying harvests? Who is your liege lord fighting against, Sir Jehan? Princes or peons?" Thibaud grunted and shot up from his seat. "Hold the sword like it's welded to your hand, boy, else your attacker will knock it out every time."

Jehan's gaze drifted to her with an indulgent half-smile. Oh, how she wished she could stand up and slip her hand in his and lead him across the hall to the stairs. Liaisons were becoming more difficult and dangerous. Perhaps she was imagining the smiling, quickly averted glances of the maidservants and the sly looks from the English men-at-arms, but in her heart she feared the worst. For Laurent's sake, she couldn't move an inch closer to the man whose touch she craved.

If only the abbot in Toulouse would respond to their messages. Jehan had already sent two, one with a peddler, and the second with a group of pilgrims, but six interminable weeks had passed with no response. She could only assume the messages were intercepted, or the monastery couldn't spare a man to return news. In either case, the silence indicated how dangerous the roads had become since the Prince of Wales had come warring. She couldn't possibly send her brother off on such roads, even with either English or French men-at-arms as guards.

Jehan kept his patience, but she sensed his bated frustration whenever she deemed it too dangerous to seek his bed. In truth, she wasn't sure she could bear this deception much longer. She wanted to embrace her new position, live openly as Jehan's lover, and stop skulking around in shame. The longer she delayed, the more likely it would be that Laurent would find out through rumor, or, worse, he'd catch them together. Then all hope for reasonable discussion would be lost.

Yes, she would take matters in her own hands.

"I got you, Rostand!" Laurent let loose a wild whoop of laughter as he swept a sweat-drenched shock of hair off his brow. "A point to me."

"And so the match is done." She stood up.

"Done?" Laurent said. "But—"

"Wasn't it you who urged me to share our extra food with the villagers?" She reached for the bowl of figs on the table before Thibaud could take another, then gestured to a platter heaped with the ends of gravy-soaked trencher bread and a few joints of quail. "Take the platter and act the monk. There will be many in the village who'll appreciate the meal."

She strode away toward the door, expecting her brother to follow. Laurent took his time about it, laying down his wooden sword, bantering with the men, and then, finally, taking the tray to do her bidding.

She pushed against the door and the winter wind slipped through the portal from the courtyard, teasing the hem of her kirtle with cold fingers.

Laurent limped down the stairs beside her, still heaving from exertion. "It's been a long time since we had enough food to deliver the remnants from our table."

"Sir Jehan is a good hunter. We'll take everything to Father Dubose, he'll know how best to distribute it."

"I don't think Thibaud was quite finished eating." He turned his eyes upon her, crinkly with humor. "What's got you frowning?"

"You," she retorted, stepping smartly toward the chapel. "Practicing swordplay with glee, like I never could get you to do before."

"An army pouring over the walls changed my perspective."

"And what happened to the wonderful monastery in Toulouse? To spending a life in spiritual contemplation?"

"That hasn't changed," he said. "But have you made *your* decision?"

"What decision?"

"Come, Ally. The whole castle is abuzz waiting for you to make up your mind. I'm not the only one who has heard you say you'd rather throw yourself off the ramparts than take the veil."

She frowned, nonplussed. "You know I'm not going to a convent."

"Ah, then you're going to marry."

She stumbled on the flagstones, righting herself

with effort. "I'm landless and without fortune, *frai*. No man in his right mind would bind himself to poverty."

"Sir Jehan has your land and your fortune. He'll marry you."

The winter wind gave a howl as it poured over the ramparts. Laurent couldn't possibly think…. But of course he did. Before she'd learned about Jehan's betrothal, she'd hoped for the same.

Suddenly, her brother scraped to a stop. He placed the platter of food on the ground, and then took the figs from her and placed them beside the platter. When he straightened up to gather her hands in his, she had to arch her neck to look into his face.

When had he become so tall?

"Aliénor, you've gone pale."

"Laurent," she said, gathering her wits, "you don't understand the situation. I'm chatelaine here. That's enough."

"You can't be chatelaine here forever. And religious life is definitely not for you. But marriage is also a sacrament—"

"Listen to you. Father would sooner see me dead than married to an Englishman."

"Father *is* probably dead."

Startled, she searched Laurent's face but saw no grief. "We don't know any such thing."

"He may as well be dead, for all the effort he's made to re-take the castle."

"Laury, it's dangerous to leap to such

conclusions. Our father is probably with the Count of Armagnac or the king himself—"

"—but he's not *here*." He tilted his head like he was confused listening to Thibaud at lessons. "Sir Jehan is strong. He's kind and generous and honorable."

She tried not to wince.

"He's a favorite of the prince and likely to be titled—"

"—with our father's *own* title."

"All the better. You'll finally be the lady of this house and not a servant within it. Free to live your life as it pleases you, in the castle that is rightfully yours."

"Laurent—"

"Before I leave here, I want to see you happy." His cheek flexed. "Before I leave, I need to know you're settled." He lowered his head to capture her gaze, and the smile that stretched on his face squeezed her heart. "He loves you, Aliénor."

Her heart did a flutter-roll in her chest.

"His gaze follows you whenever you're in the room. His voice changes when he talks to you."

She stared at their entwined hands. With every bone in her body she wanted to believe what her brother said, but she couldn't trust her own heart, never mind the conclusions of a man-boy too innocent of the ways of the world.

"Love in marriage is an unexpected gift, so I'm told." He pulled her into a brotherly hug. "Don't scorn it."

She laid her head against her brother's shoulder, breathing in the lingering scent of frankincense in the woolen fibers of his tunic from the morning's Mass, as well as the faintly unpleasant stink of him, sweaty from sparring. All through their lives, she had been the one to offer Laurent kind words and comfort. How strong he had grown in the past year, strong and true and full of goodness, and suddenly she couldn't bear telling him a truth that would destroy his happiness.

Her courage, what there was of it, flew away like a flock of sparrows in October.

"I haven't made my decision yet," she mumbled against his shoulder, despising herself for lying. "I'll send word to you after you're settled in the monastery."

"No."

"Laury—"

"I promised you I wouldn't leave until I've drunk a glass of wine at your wedding."

"But so much is uncertain. We don't know if father lives, or if the prince will give Jehan this castle."

"I'm staying." He turned, swept up the figs and the platter. "I don't care how long it takes. The monastery can wait."

"Laurent, this is just stubborn foolishness. I insist—"

"Insist all you want, but I intend to be the one who gives you away at the church steps, Ally." He grinned, showing a slight chip in his front tooth. "Even if I have to battle Thibaud for the honor."

***

Jehan watched her.

He watched, on Twelfth Night, as she swathed herself in a cloak and mounted a mare to invite the villagers to the castle. He watched as she returned with a crowd in her wake, making a racket with reed pipes and skin-drums, weaving up the steep path to the castle carrying tallow-drenched torches while Aliénor, wearing a coronet of woven ivy, dismounted and danced like some woodland fairy. Aliénor threw open the door. The mead hall was still festooned with garlands of Christmas greenery. She invited in the crowd, offering a feast generous with both food and wine.

The meal was merry, and just as it was finished she summoned a few villagers to blow music through their reed-pipes. Soon there was clapping and dancing and, for the children, games of hoodman blind. He watched her weave through the crowded room, made warm from torches, the hearth fire, and the close proximity of so many bodies, keeping an eye on possible trouble as she dodged the reach of drunken men-at-arms while checking pitchers for fullness.

She was a sorceress, conjuring the season to life, filling the castle with the greatest of cheer. He scraped back his chair where he sat in supposed majesty, stood up unsteadily, and plunged into the crowd so he wouldn't be the only man in the room who hadn't danced with her. When he finally came upon her, he wound an arm around her waist and pulled her back against his body.

She smelled of pine and new wine and woman, and she giggled as if she'd had one cup too many.

"Jehan," she whispered, grasping his forearm, "you shouldn't—"

"It's Twelfth Night. I could strip you bare on the stairs, take you as I will, and no one would raise a brow."

"You," she said, "are exaggerating."

"Every other man in this room has embraced you, touched you, or danced at your side. Am I to be the only one denied?"

She whispered, "My brother—"

"—has gone to the chapel to pray for all our souls."

He'd seen the boy leave, uneasy with the revelry, looking aghast at all the wild eyes and drunken laughter.

"Besides," he added, burying his face in her soft hair, "there's not a sober eye in all the room. No one will notice if we leave."

It had been two days and several hours since their last coupling, a furtive thing, a stolen moment in his tower room under the pretense of arranging the meal for the feast, with Esquival outside the door on watch.

His cock stiffened with the need to feel her body against his. To feel, if only for a moment, that this was not an interval with a beginning and an end, but one moment in a long lifetime.

"I'll leave first," she whispered. "Meet me in my room."

She flashed a bright gaze over her shoulder before she disappeared amid the crowd. He found his way to the hearth and stared into the flames, counting the moments, trying his best not to imagine the sound of her gasp in his ear, the undulation of her slim, strong body beneath his. Then he was stepping over kissing couples as he climbed the stairs to the upper floor.

The torches had sputtered out, leaving the second floor gallery in darkness. He clung to the shadows as he passed her brother's empty room and set as his goal the faint, orange glow spilling out from beneath her door, neatly ajar.

Ensuring no eyes were upon him, he slipped in and closed it behind him. A quick glance around the room showed her maidservant was not here, likely enjoying the revelries below and ordered to continue to do so. The drapes of the bed had been drawn. He approached and yanked them aside.

Aliénor lay propped against the pillows, her dark blonde hair, bronzed in the flickering light, spread across the pale linen. Blood roared in his ears as he drank in the sight of her, wearing nothing but a smile.

"I've been waiting so long." Her voice was

husky. "I was starting to think you preferred Thibaud's company to mine."

He dug a knee into the bed and pulled her into his arms, breathing in the smell of pine and woman.

"If Rudel had grabbed you one more time," he murmured as he pressed his forehead against hers. "I was going to draw a sword."

"Rudel was drunk, he grabbed at every woman."

"No, he was fixed on you."

"Hush." Her hands ran over his back, soft as a breeze. "I am blind to all men but you."

With a groan he pulled away long enough to yank off his clothes, tossing them at the end of the bed before climbing in.

"Pull the drapes," she whispered, drawing him close.

"I want to see you." He filled his hand with her breast. "I want to watch your face when you—"

"Jehan."

Her gaze was steady and determined, one brow lifted in expectation of obedience. She wound her arms around his neck. "Pull the drapes, my love."

He'd seen this look on her face when she chastised servants lagging in their duties. How he looked forward to a night when the risk of discovery wouldn't linger between them, bringing the stain of shame to something that did not in the least feel shameful.

With a grunt he jerked the linen hangings closed. No sooner had he done so when she pressed against him so her breasts softened upon his chest. Desire flavored her kiss. He wanted to take his time, to touch her until she writhed under his hand. Running his tongue across her bottom lip, he slipped his fingers between her thighs. She let them fall open. His fingertips slid inside her and she quivered at his touch.

But then her hand was on his hip, pressuring him so he would slide between her legs as she wriggled into a better position. He removed his hand from where he stroked her and shifted his weight evenly on either side of her body. She let out a soft gasp as his cock kissed her cleft. Before he could stop her, she pushed up against his shaft so she took inside her the warm head.

"God's Blood, Aliénor," he rasped, his teeth gritted.

All his well-made plans for a slow, long lovemaking, all the wicked, glorious things he intended to do with her, they would have to wait. Instead, he gave in to his aching cock and filled her with one swift plunge.

Her cry of pleasure made his heart leap.

Her fingers dug into his hips as he withdrew a fraction before plunging deeper. She arched beneath him, making breathy little noises. He ran his hand down her side to palm the fullness of one buttock, lifting her hips to meet his with the next hungry thrust. She gasped as their loins pressed tight. He couldn't see her well, not with the drapes drawn tight, but he imagined the flush rising on her face, the parting of her lips, the ecstacy crossing her face.

This lovemaking felt primitive and unstoppable. He tightened his will to take care, not lose control. He nearly lost it when she whispered his name in rising desperation before shuddering against him like a silk pennon in the wind.

He buried his face in her shoulder, holding himself back until her strong spasms gentled. Only then did he make his last strong strokes before he pulled himself out. His own passion exploded and he released his seed into the linens.

Moments later, he muttered in her ear, "I'm always taking you like a man who hasn't had a woman in years."

Her throaty laugh seemed to ripple through the air. He ran his fingers through her unbound hair, spreading the tresses across the furs. He wiped the perspiration from the nape of her neck and then slipped off her body to lie at her side.

A draft moved amid the folds of the drapes. A slivered opening let in a slim shaft of pale light. For a long time, he gazed at her in that dusky light, waiting for those soft, gilded brown eyes to finally blink open.

When they did, she turned her face and her smile lit up the space between them.

His heart squeezed.

We winter in Bordeaux, the prince had said.

How much longer did he dare stay at her side?

***

Aliénor woke to the sound of her chamber door banging open.

"Ally! I have a message from the abbot at Toulouse!"

She grunted at her brother's voice and curled into herself. Her mouth felt as dry as the lees of last night's spiced wine. She heard the whoosh of the bed curtains being knocked aside as light flooded over her.

"He invited me," he said in that pummeling voice, "to join the order as soon as I can get there."

"Laury, for the love of Mary." She raised a hand to shield her eyes. "What ungodly hour is it?"

"Long past when you should be awake—"

Laurent's words halted with a wet, glottal sound. Assuming she was exposed, she clasped at the furs and pulled them higher. If her lark of a brother was embarrassed by her nudity, then so be it. It was no more than he deserved barging in on her like this. And on the morning after Twelfth Night, no less.

Then she shot up to a sitting position, a move made difficult by the naked arm lying heavy across her waist.

"So," her brother said in a high, strained voice. "Now I understand why you lingered abed."

"Laury, I can explain." She licked her dry lips with a sandpaper tongue as she struggled to adjust to the brightness of day. "Twelfth Night is—"

"Please don't." He raised the flat of his hand. "It's enough for me that you've finally made your decision."

Words gathered in her throat but she couldn't muster them to her lips.

"You'll have to say penance, of course, the two of you, but this won't be the first time a bedding was made before the wedding."

Her brother stood before her with a shaky half-smile on his face, flushing crimson to the roots of his hair.

He didn't understand, she thought, her heart sinking.

He didn't understand at all.

Then the warm mass of the naked man in her bed moved behind her, jiggling the hay-stuffed mattress.

"I confess, Sir Jehan," her brother said, raising his voice as if Jehan stood across the room instead of supine on the bed behind her, "I'd expected better of you, but I suppose my sister needed some…convincing."

Jehan's warmth shifted as he sat up behind her and placed a gentle hand on her shoulder. "You said you received a message, Laurent?"

"Yes, yes." Her brother lifted the folded parchment and stared at it as his skin began to blotch. "It arrived with a peddler from Toulouse."

"Any other messages?"

They're talking about messages, she thought,

while she lay naked in bed with her lover.

"None but this." Laury waved the thing so it kicked up a breeze. "My news will be overshadowed by yours, but happily so."

"So," Jehan persisted, "you'll be going to the monastery."

"And this shall make my leave-taking all the more joyous." He took a trip-step backwards toward the door. "I'll speak to Father Dubose about the arrangements for the ceremony. It can take place before breakfast—"

"No!" She'd all but shouted the word.

"Would you prefer a midday ceremony, Ally?" He gave her a sweet tilt of the head, as he dragged his leg along. "Because the time for hesitation is clearly past."

"I made my choice some time ago."

"Then why didn't you say anything?" Laurent paused and spread his hands.

She ached for a cup of wine, as much for fortitude's sake as thirst. With a squeeze of her shoulder, Jehan reached for his clothes, rumpled at the end of the bed, and slipped through the drapes on the other side. He was trying to give them some privacy, she supposed, for she'd told Jehan from the start that Laurent would have to hear the truth from her lips alone. But bereft of his warmth, her will faltered, while every silent moment stole another measure of brightness from her brother's face.

Clutching furs to her chest, she said, "There can

be no wedding, *frai*.”

“Nonsense. There will be a marriage before dinner today.”

“Prince Edward has put Sir Jehan under obligations.” She found her chemise amid the furs. ““These obligations prevent him from making any other…attachments.” She searched for the neck-hole of her chemise, holding furs close to her body until the linen covered her.

Laurent switched his attention to Jehan, who came around the bed buckling his belt. “Tell me you will marry her.”

Jehan said, “I shall make arrangements.”

“See?” Laurent grinned at her anew. “I told you—”

“Arrangements,” Jehan interrupted, “for you to leave for the monastery this very day.”

“*After* the wedding.”

“I will send two of my men to guard you.” Jehan’s words were low and calm, as if he were murmuring to an unbroken colt. “The roads are still dangerous.”

Laurent shook his head, his black eyes narrowing, and a look came over his face that made her heart falter.

Laury said, “You will marry my sister.”

A muscle moved in Jehan’s cheek. “If it were in my power, I would wed your sister this hour.”

“Then *do so*.”

“Prince Edward has arranged a betrothal with

someone else."

Laurent's face went ashen-white. He took one step forward to seize a handful of Jehan's shirt with a fist.

"It was my choice," she said, swinging her legs out from under the covers before her brother did anything foolish. "*My* choice, Laury."

"How could it have been a choice," he argued, "when there is no alternative?"

"I could have refused him." She stepped toward the men. "I offered myself of my own free will. I'd be lying if I pretended otherwise."

"You," her brother said, throwing the word in Jehan's face, "promised to protect her."

"That will never change."

"This is your vengeance against my father. You've turned my sister into a—"

"Careful," Jehan interrupted. "I won't abide disrespect to her, even from her own brother."

With one swift move, Jehan knocked Laurent's grip away sharply. Startled, she looked from one to the other, glaring hard at each other.

They both loved her. They both wanted the best for her.

"Come with me, Ally," Laurent said in a soft, oddly calm voice. "There's a convent alongside the monastery."

"Go to the monastery with my blessing, *frai.*" She swallowed against the tightness of her throat. "I am staying here."

He took a stumbling step back. Her ribs squeezed until she could hardly breathe. The look he gave her cut her to the quick.

She stared at her feet so she would not have to witness him leaving, though she couldn't help but hear the drag of his foot as he headed toward the door. Whether she chose a convent or a leman's bed, she supposed she'd always known she would lose one of them.

"Ally."

She forced her chin up. Framed by the doorway, Laury gave her one last, inscrutable look.

"I always knew I would have to save you from yourself."

CHAPTER FOURTEEN

"How can this be, Jehan?"
From the hurt in her voice, Jehan knew that Aliénor didn't want an answer—at least not an honest one. She still hadn't lifted her gaze from the parchment trembling in her hands as she re-read it by the light of the hearth fire. It was a missive from Toulouse, confirming not for the first time that Aliénor's brother had never arrived at the monastery gates.

"All these months," she murmured, refolding the parchment. "Where could he possibly be?"

The sadness and anxiety had returned to her voice. She kept running her fingers along the parchment seams. Having spent the long, gray months of winter living as her husband in all but name, he had prided himself on thinking he'd helped subsume her feelings of grief and guilt about

Laurent's reckless departure. Mostly by holding and kissing and touching her until her face bloomed with as much joy as he felt, being the man she chose to love.

Yet, watching her now, he couldn't help but wonder. Would she be as sad and anxious if the missive in her hand were exchanged for the one crinkling in his pocket, the message from the prince demanding his presence in Bordeaux?

She said, "We must find him, Jehan."

He exchanged a glance with Thibaud, sitting grimly across the trestle table, and then just as quickly looked away.

Thibaud clanked his cup on the trestle table. "You won't find your brother now."

"We can't do nothing."

"Woman, after he took off on his own, we searched every bastide from Pavie to Mirande. We asked at every monastery, every village, and every church in between, while riding on Lenten rations, sleeping in the coldest rain—" Thibaud closed his mouth and sighed hard through his nose. "He left after Twelfth Night and now it's past Easter. He could be halfway to Rome."

She turned on Thibaud. "He's wearing a nobleman's clothes—any brigand would have noticed. Even the worst of sell-swords wouldn't just—"

Aliénor's wild gaze traveled to him and then skittered away. She knew, he thought, but she couldn't bear the thought. Months missing, yet no ransom demand had arrived. And now, with the turning of Easter, armies were gathering, both French and English, taking sell-swords into their ranks and clearing the roads of the worst of dangers. If sell-swords or brigands wanted to ransom a young Tournan, they'd have come to Castelnau long since. All during the month they searched, Jehan and Thibaud and his men hadn't been seeking the angry young man who had left his sister so distraught.

They'd searched for a corpse.

With a scrape of her heel, she turned back to the hearth. The light of the flames cast a halo around her. Thibaud looked to him, his bushy brows pushed high. Like Laurent, Thibaud hadn't been happy with the arrangement between Jehan and Aliénor, but Thibaud was a man of the world. His rheumy eyes followed the two of them always, and now, Thibaud's pointed look said it was Jehan's responsibility to comfort Thibaud's distraught kinswoman.

Jehan shoved his goblet of wine away and swung his legs over the bench to join her at the hearth.

From behind he gripped her shoulders. She sank her head back upon his chest with a sigh that seemed to emerge from the bottom of her lungs.

"He's not dead, Jehan."

He pressed his lips into her hair. "You have great faith to believe so."

"I *know* so." Beneath his palms her shoulders trembled. "When Laury was little, I knew when something was wrong. When he fell off his pony on his tenth birthday, I felt the bruise in my own side. When he defied our father, the terror I experienced was an echo of his own. If Laurent were dead," she said, tapping her breast with the fist still gripping the parchment, "I would know it *here*."

"Then you have nothing to worry about."

"I've already lost two brothers," she whispered. "Bertrand. Gaston."

He knew they'd died during the plague. She'd whispered stories about them to him during the dark winter mornings, when lovemaking had made them languid.

"I cannot bear the thought," she murmured, "of losing the only one I have left."

He wrapped his arms around her shoulders, holding her close, wishing he could dispel these shadows. But for this loss, their life had become a wonder: A series of calm, ordered days followed by warm, sweet evenings. How he loved the lazy breaking of fast in their bed, crumbs from fresh-baked loaves falling into the linens. Their joy seemed to spread throughout the castle, for the maidservants bustled, gossiping, in the buttery, the men-at-arms laughed as they sparred in the courtyard or cleaned their chain-mail by the fire while the fragrance of the oil filled the air. Plain but hearty dinners lingered for hours as the light sifting through the arrow-slits waned, with Aliénor sitting by the fire, bent over needlework with the flames making gold of her hair.

All his life he'd wanted nothing more than peace

and security for himself and his men, without really knowing what that meant beyond food in their bellies, strong walls keeping them safe, a roof above their head, and the warmth of a fire. He had not really known what it meant until he took this woman as his own. This was what kept him in Castelnau despite the duty that now lay in his pocket.

"Ride with me today," he said. Her heart was always light after she'd raced over the hills. "You can bring your sparrow hawk."

"How I would love to." She slipped her soft hand over his forearm. "But today is the first Monday of the month. You must mete out justice to your vassals."

He'd forgotten. Every month he sat in the carved oak chair as one villager after another argued about whose chicken belonged to whom and who'd slaughtered someone else's goat. Personally he thought it would be more efficient to distribute swords among the garrulous peasants and allow them to settle their differences in blood, but he knew he should value an existence where the worst trouble was whether someone had moved a border stone one step deeper into someone else's holding.

"Perhaps after," she said, mustering a brave little smile. "A ride on the hills would be lovely, now that the weather is turning."

He sifted a curl of her golden hair between his fingers, tempted to kiss the lingering sadness from her lips.

He was halfway there when the door to the courtyard burst open.

"My lord!" Esquival raced in. "Armed men are riding toward the castle."

Jehan barked, "How many?"

"Two dozen, at least."

"I'm coming."

Jehan followed his squire into the courtyard with Aliénor at his heels, his uneasiness rising. He hadn't told her about the parchment he'd received, the direct order to come to the prince's side. It would be just like the prince to send a dozen men to demand obedience, to escort him to his liege lord to take punishment for insubordination.

On the ramparts, he saw the guards staring off to the east. Cloudy skies cast a pale gray glow over the greening hills of Gascony, but no fog concealed the approach of the group of armed men. One look at the hard-riding group and Jehan breathed a sigh of relief. Only a few wore armor bright enough to gleam in the dim light. The others rode without helmets; their horses bare of war trappings.

Not the prince's men, of that he was sure.

"Esquival," he commanded, knowing that his young squire had the sharpest vision. "Can you make out the symbols on the pennant?"

Esquival leaned between the crenellations to get a better look at the approaching men. Aliénor, tense with apprehension, clutched Jehan's arm.

"I see it, my lord," Esquival said. "I see the

colors."

"My God," she said breathlessly, leaning dangerously over the ramparts while the wind tossed her hair, "I see him!"

Then Jehan noticed, too, the twisted foot of the forward rider who carried high the pennant of Tournan.

CHAPTER FIFTEEN

Aliénor kept blinking to clear her sight. Laurent's arrival must be a cruel trick of her mind, an image conjured up from months of worry and anguish and dwindling hope. But no matter how many times she rubbed her eyes, Laurent was still there, riding toward the bridge to the village.

Relief flooded through her like a spring melt. She leaned into Jehan and filled her lungs with the scent of smoke, iron, and leather rising from the fibers of his surcoat. "I was so afraid I'd never see him again."

Laurent's disappearance had been the one cloud in her heart these past months, the only blot on her happiness.

"Thibaud," Jehan shouted above her head. "Greet them and find out what they want."

Something in Jehan's voice gave her pause. She pulled away to look up at him, his jaw stony, his expression dark.

"You'll pay the ransom," she said. "You promised."

"I will pay any ransom, *couret*." He looked at her with a knot between his brows. "If your brother is indeed a prisoner of those men."

"Of course he is."

"A prisoner doesn't ride ahead of his captors."

His words gave her pause. She'd been so happy to see Laurent's familiar silhouette that she hadn't given mind to anything else.

An impossible thought passed through her mind but she dismissed it as foolishness.

"My brother must have been ordered to ride in front so you would recognize him," she argued. "Otherwise, you might shoot the sell-swords full of arrows at their approach."

"A prisoner doesn't bear his own standard."

"Again," she said, her heart doing a little skip-dance against her ribs, "they made him carry it so you would recognize—"

"—the force behind him," Jehan interrupted softly. "Following in his wake."

"That's no army." She could no longer see the mounted men, presumably already on the cliff side path up to the castle. "I saw only a small band of men armed with pikes—"

"Men-at-arms," he corrected. "Some wearing chain mail, others boiled leather jerkins."

"Like many a sell-sword wanting ransom for a

noble prisoner."

"Aliénor."

"This is *Laurent*, Jehan. My saintly brother, bound for the monastery. What else could this be about?"

She met those stark blue eyes, sharp with concern, willing him to see sense.

"He'll be greeted at the gate," Jehan said, "and asked his business. Pray, Aliénor, he hasn't done anything foolish."

Jehan turned to stride the dozen yards to the ramparts at the front of the castle, where, by the sound of horses and men, the contingent had just emerged over the rise into the clearing. A sudden squeal of rope and gears spurred her into action, and she joined Jehan above the portal just as the drawbridge was lowered.

Her brother kicked his mount close without hesitation. He wore no helmet and the wind tossed his shock of dark hair. The winter had frozen the softness off him—his cheeks were lean, and his surcoat stretched tight across a chest wider than she remembered. That surcoat bore an approximation of the Tournan eagle, probably sewn with his own clumsy hand. Despite her apprehension, her heart soared to see him healthy, when for months she'd been imagining him abused and beaten by brigands or thieves, half-starved on the hillsides.

Yet, at the same time, the ease at which he pulled his horse to a stop in the middle of the field, while his men formed a semicircle behind him, made her ribs squeeze tight.

The portcullis creaked open. She look down to see the top of Thibaud's spun-wool head as her great-uncle rode across the drawbridge to meet her brother. She pressed her body between the crenellations, straining to catch fragments of the conversation, but all she could hear was Thibaud speaking in a fierce tone with ever-rising animation while Laurent shook his head with a strange calm.

In the midst of Thibaud's rant, her brother lifted his face. It was no longer as pale as the moon, that face. It had been darkened by sunshine and chapped by wind and there were hollows around his eyes. Yet this was unmistakably Laurent, her little brother, and the half-smile he gave her was rueful, sad.

Her stomach began to churn. Why did the armed men stand in a semicircle at a distance, watching the ramparts? Why didn't Laurent dismount from his horse and embrace his great-uncle as he should? Where was the leader of these brigands, stepping forward, asking for ransom? And why was Jehan standing beside her as still as a stone statue, frowning at it all?

Her mind balked at the only explanation she could conceive. There must be another, there had to be.

Thibaud finally yanked his horse around and cantered back into the castle, dismounting in the courtyard with a jangle of reins. His steps fell upon the stairs to the ramparts with grim force as he climbed up to join them.

When he emerged, Jehan barked, "Well?"

Thibaud's face was like stone, etched deep. "It is as we both feared."

Jehan spoke a curse she'd never heard fall from his lips, an expletive like a knife-tip slicing across her hopes.

"Remember," Thibaud ventured, holding up a hand, "my great-nephew is but a boy—"

"He's no boy, Thibaud."

"Fifteen years of age hardly qualifies—"

"At fifteen," Jehan interrupted, "I fended for myself in the hills of Gascony. At fifteen, the Prince of Wales was knighted at Crécy. At fifteen, my brother—"

"You were all raised as knights," Thibaud argued. "But my kinsman is a cripple, raised only for the church."

"And yet your monk-cripple has led a band of armed men to my gates. Did I send the wrong man to do my bidding?"

Thibaud flushed and pressed his beard against his chest.

"Stop making excuses," Jehan insisted, "and *speak.*"

Aliénor flattened her hand against her chest as if to hold in the heart threatening to beat out of her skin.

With a harsh sigh, her uncle said, "My kinsman

claims, in the absence of his father, he is acting as the true heir of this castle."

Laurent!

"He claims," Thibaud continued, "you are an English usurper. It is his intent to remove you from this place."

"My brother doesn't want this castle." All attention turned to her, but Jehan's sharp gaze struck her breathless. "Laury doesn't want the title. He never has."

"The situation has changed, little dove."

The endearment was meant to calm her, but his gentle words were no match against his fierce gaze.

She turned to her great-uncle in search of common sense. "Thibaud, how is my brother to seize this castle with so few men?"

"Through force of honor. Based on his rightful claim."

"Force of honor does not carry weapons." Hot blood rose to her cheeks. "He is outmanned, and we're behind stone walls."

Thibaud barked, "I told him the same."

"There's the proof he's acting out of desperation—he doesn't know what he's doing."

"He knows what he's doing." The creases in Thibaud's face deepened as he turned his attention to Jehan. "My great-nephew sees no solution except in your death, Sir Jehan, or his own."

A relentless pulse pounded on her temple. *Laury, Laury, what are you thinking?*

Jehan murmured, "He knows I won't kill him."

"That's why he's challenging you to single combat."

CHAPTER SIXTEEN

Jehan said, "Come with me, Aliénor."

Aliénor felt so numb she didn't notice Jehan's grip on her arm until she was halfway down the stairs. The fabric of her slippers caught on the rough surface of the stones, making her stumble. Only when they emerged into the courtyard, when the weight of a hundred stares struck her, did she manage to summon a measure of dignity to shake free of Jehan's grip.

They entered the donjon, passed through the great hall, and climbed the stairs all the way up to his tower room. There, Jehan shut the door behind them.

She blurted, "He doesn't know what he's doing, Jehan."

He yanked his surcoat over his head. "His message was clear enough." He balled the cloth and tossed it with force into a corner.

"He's still a child—"

"A boy who gathers men-at-arms to fight under his banner is no longer a child."

A scuff of a foot startled her and she realized they were not alone. His squire, Esquival, approached with a padded doublet in his hands. Jehan shoved his arms through the armholes of the garment.

Jehan was putting on armor.

"This is nonsense," she whispered, as her heart skittered like a frightened mouse and the words *single combat* and *fight to the death* rang in her head. "There are hardly enough men to threaten the castle—"

"And yet," he interrupted, while his squire laced the garment, "too many to ignore."

"You could capture them, subdue them, and put an end to this without—"

"Not without killing one or more. Think, Aliénor. How did your brother recruit those men?"

She shook her head, pressing fingers against an ache in her temple. She couldn't fathom what had happened over the long, cold winter to change Laury so much that he would emerge three months later to challenge a seasoned knight.

"Do you think he promised them gold, riches?" Jehan persisted.

"No." She swallowed. "He wouldn't pillage his own home." *Or put himself in the path of her lover's sword.*

"Does he think he can control them if they were to breach these walls?"

"He would never put me in harm's way, or any

of his people."

"How else do you lure sell-swords and mercenaries?" He tied off the ends of the laces as his squire fetched his chain-mail shirt. "What else do you offer them but plunder?"

The prickling of fear at the back of her neck tightened into a cold, painful knot.

"Those men who follow your brother," he continued, "were probably starving on the hills when he met them. Wondering where their next meal was coming from, or when the next war would start up so they might sleep under canvas again."

She ceased pacing. Once, in the middle of a cold night, she'd woken up to catch him staring blindly at the wooden beams of this tower-roof. *Sometimes,* he'd said, *I still think I'm sleeping on the hard ground with a hungry belly and the cold freezing my blood.*

"But if I were a sell-sword who'd come upon your brother," he murmured, "I could be talked into fighting for him."

She blinked, nonplussed. "Why?"

"To regain pride," he said. "For a chance to fight for a rightful cause."

She pressed a finger to her temple harder as Esquival carried the heavy chain-mail tunic to his master. "You're making this sound like a crusade."

"Exactly."

"Except he doesn't want the castle, the lands, the title—"

"He's not doing it for the lands." Jehan fixed his

blue, blue eyes upon her. "He's doing this for *you,* Aliénor."

The only sound in the room was the ringing of chain-mail links as he ducked his head into the neck-hole and the garment unfurled to the top of his thighs. She took a step back, and then another, until the edge of the new bed struck the back of her knees.

Denial was a lie she could not push through the tightening of her throat. She sat down on the bed and pressed her palms against the hay-stuffed mattress. She and Jehan had spent the cold morning here, making their own warmth under its linens. But for Laurent's disappearance, she had been happier in the past months than she had ever been. This was the life she'd always craved, a home and hearth of her own, and a good man to share it with.

Love was something she'd never dared hoped for, a blessing beyond all her wishes.

Now she gathered the links of her belt in her hand and squeezed until they bit into her palm. "If my brother has come to save me from dishonor," she said, "then his cause is more misguided than I imagined."

"Not so misguided." He twisted to tie his chain mail-hose as his squire buckled his chausses on his feet. "If I were your brother, I would have done the same."

She heard the frustration in his words, as well as something else—gruff, unreadable, unnerving.

"I told him," she said, "this was my choice."

"I heard every word, *couret.*"

A muscle in his jaw flexed in the way it did when a matter vexed him to distraction. She'd lain in bed many a night watching that face, knowing when something bothered him, whether it was due to an issue as small as a theft of a lamb or as complicated as brokering a peace between two villagers arguing over the positioning of a border stone. If the matter threatened to steel sleep from him, she would press her lips against his brow, take his head in her hands, and lead him to pleasure and bliss.

She pushed up from the bed. "Enough, Esquival," she said, as the squire slipped the surcoat over Jehan's head. "I shall finish the task."

Jehan nodded at his squire as he wrestled his arms through the sleeves. Esquival bowed and slipped out the door.

Her fingers trembled as she approached. She searched for the loose laces on the side of his surcoat, conscious of the intensity of his gaze. She pulled upon the laces as if she were pulling her wits together.

"Perhaps I have been blind." Her voice came out in a whisper though no one else was in the room. "Laury is my youngest sibling, and I have spent a lifetime protecting him. I have only ever seen him as a boy."

She felt the warmth of his perusal.

"Clearly," she added, fumbling to tie the last lace, "you understand my brother better than me. Perhaps, then, you can find a way to convince him to give up this madness, without a terrible dangerous fight."

"*Couret,* he's as stubborn as you."

"But not as clever as *you.* After all, you managed, with the prince's help, to seize a castle that's never before been taken."

"If your father hadn't abandoned it, the outcome might have been different."

"Still," she said, moving to his other side, to the other laces, "your influence with the prince assured that this castle, and the village, weren't burnt to the ground."

He gave her a curious frown, as if he hadn't expected her to guess he was the cause. Yet everyone in the castle had heard the reports that the prince had burned a swath from Seissan to Narbonne, skipping right over them. If he could outwit a prince, surely he could outwit a boy…or a young man.

"And since then," she continued, "you've managed to stay in this castle three full months longer than the Prince of Wales wanted."

She did not have to look up to know his gaze had intensified.

"I'm your chatelaine," she explained. "Do you think a single message arrives at this castle without me knowing of it?"

"I took it from the messenger's own hand, and then sent him on his way."

"A large, mud-splattered horse at the gate? Bearing a dagged-edged blanket beneath its saddle, and a fine leather pouch at its side? I see everything,

Jehan, and what I miss, the kitchen servants report."

"Is a man not master of his own castle?"

"It's my task to make you believe so."

A grin flittered across his face. She let her fingers linger on the trailing leather tie, hoping he would put his arms around her, kiss her, reassure her, but his smile faded as quickly as it had come.

"My point," she said, feeling the absence of his touch like an ache, "is you are older, better trained, and more experienced than my brother. Certainly you can trick a fifteen-year-old boy into surrendering without a battle?"

He pulled a fraction away. "You'd rather I trick your brother than have him fight like a knight?"

"He belongs in a monastery." She pressed her palm against his chest, feeling the weave of the wool and the ripple of chain mail beneath. "Don't make him pay dearly for a misguided cause."

He ran a bare finger down her cheek. When it reached her chin he tilted her face up to meet his. "He would make me his executioner."

"But you won't kill him—"

"He would rip me out of your heart."

"That's not possible," she said huskily, "if you refuse to fight him."

She tried to read the changing expressions on his face, desperate to see some sign of agreement.

Jehan stepped away in silence. The fabric of his surcoat slipped across her palm, the green and blue embroidery shimmering in the dim light.

Her brother and her lover would be wearing the same colors.

"You won't fight him," she blurted, clinging to hope.

She heard a clatter as Jehan took his sword belt in hand.

CHAPTER SEVENTEEN

This was a battle he could not win.

Jehan mounted his horse and pounded across the drawbridge, a dozen men-at-arms in his wake. He didn't have to glance up to know Aliénor stood upon the ramparts like a carved wooden doll. When he'd left her in their tower bedroom, her soft, dark eyes had begged him for hope.

He covered the short distance across the field to where Laurent sat astride a war horse. Curious villagers had made their way up the hill to cluster at the edge of the clearing, not far from where the muddy earth gave way to the limestone cliff. Laurent remained astride his horse, his motley army arrayed behind him, his bad foot at an awkward angle in the stirrup.

Jehan walked his horse so close their mounts were snout to snout. "Ride away from this place,

Laurent, and you will live."

"My uncle said much the same thing."

The boy's face had grown lean, dark at the jaw with a patchy shadow of beard. A livid scar cut across one cheek. The black eyes that met his were so like the boy's father, except the expression in them was both sad and full of grim humor.

No longer a child, indeed.

"I will pay your men." Jehan spoke clearly enough so the sell-swords would hear him. "Your debt to them will be absolved."

"I owe them nothing but my gratitude. You can't pay that back in the same coin."

The boy spoke with a calm confidence, confirming Jehan's worst fears. "So you've spurned the monastery."

"The church will get me, by and by." The boy turned his head, squinting toward the far hills. "In a long, pine box, most likely."

Jehan tightened his grip on the reins, less to still his restless mount and more to gain time to decide whether the boy's flippant attitude was bravado, or something graver and more disturbing.

Jehan said, "You're outmatched."

"I suspect so."

"In the face of a stronger force, there's no shame in conceding."

"Do you know what shame is, Sir Jehan?"

Jehan's jaw went tight. His mind flashed on Aliénor standing in the moonlight wearing nothing but a shift, offering herself to him with no promise of marriage. And he, taking her gift, knowing he could propose nothing honorable in return.

"*I* know everything about shame," the boy continued, resting his arms on the pommel of his saddle. "My father beat it into me as often as he could."

"Your father is not an example to follow."

"And that's precisely why I'm here. Because my father is *not*."

"Your cause isn't valid. Your father disowned you long before I seized this castle."

Laurent shrugged. "You know my real reason for being here."

"She is in agony right now, watching this."

The boy didn't spare a glance toward the ramparts. "I know."

"Ease her pain. Leave."

"I ask the same of you."

"Your sister," he said, speaking through his teeth, "wants me to stay."

"Does she wish me to leave?"

Jehan remembered her rush of relief upon recognizing her brother riding home across the fields, then bit down his growing frustration. "She will not thank you for this, Laurent."

"Not at first." He pushed up from the pommel. Light flashed off his arm braces as he swung his lame foot over his horse. "She may never forgive me. But my sister deserves to have someone fighting for her.

In the absence of my damned coward of a father, that someone will be me."

The boy hit the ground with surprising grace. One of his pike men stepped forward to lead the steed away. Laurent pulled his sword from its scabbard, swinging it in a full circle by the hilt before gripping it in two hands, waiting.

Jehan remembered Aliénor's hand on his chest.

You won't fight him, Jehan.

He breathed hard through his nose. The boy wasn't giving him any choice but to go through with this mockery of a challenge. He eyeballed Laurent's armor, saw the outline of some kind of padded, plated doublet beneath his surcoat. Yet the young fool wore no mailed hose, no chain-mail coif. No helmet. The boy's mismatched feet were braced, his grip on the hilt firm.

Damn it.

Jehan dismounted. He yanked off his chain-mail gauntlets and tossed them aside. His helm joined them with a clatter. He crouched to pinch the buckles on his chausses, intending to bring some sort of parity to this contest.

"*Enough,*" Laurent said and then started toward him, a lurching blur. Jehan fell to one knee as he grasped the hilt of his sword, pulling it free in time to stop the boy's angular swing. The clash of metal rang across the clearing, not so loud as to drown out Aliénor's scream.

Beyond their crossed swords, Laurent's face

darkened in determination. Lunging to his feet, Jehan shoved the boy. Then he fixed his stance and gripped his sword to give the boy a moment to regain his balance.

Laurent found his feet faster than expected.

Jehan said, "You've been training."

"Harder than ever."

Laurent lunged again. The boy's uneven gait made predicting the arc of his sword-swing tricky, but Jehan parried without a pause. He brought his sword around and knocked Laurent's out of his way, opening the boy's torso to attack, but Laurent lurched to his good side more quickly than his crooked leg seemed to allow—then dropped to roll upon the ground and lay a sharp, flat-sided blow to Jehan's chain-mail hose.

Jehan recoiled a step, the metal links ringing. He slammed the flat of his sword on the boy's bent back. A whistling noise alerted him to a blade slicing through air, a blow he jerked to avoid but not before it cut a welt through the embroidery of his surcoat.

Jehan frowned at the frayed fabric, surprised at Laurent's sly, effective feint.

Jehan had intended to make this fight look fierce, to draw some blood and to give some of his own as well. It would be cruel to shame Aliénor's brother in front of his men-at-arms and the villagers who once looked upon this young Tournan as the future lord. But he didn't expect the young cripple to be trained enough to *earn* his ounce of pride.

Jehan narrowed his focus grimly.

The boy wanted a real fight.

He swung his sword and the vibration of the clash shuddered to his shoulder. The boy had been trained to use not just his arms but the bulk of his body to hold firm. Jehan swung away and returned at a different angle, again and again, testing Laurent's favored side for weakness. The boy stood firm when he could, took a few steps back when pressed, and slid his sword down to release it from a hold when he grew weary.

Jehan shifted his attention, eyeing the way Laurent maneuvered his crippled foot to better predict the direction of the next attack. He struck hard, pushed in the boy's weaker direction, but the boy slid his sword free like water through a sluice. Jehan used the landscape of this muddy field to nudge his opponent toward rocks that formed tripping hazards all across the ground, but the boy must have remembered the location of each one, because he danced over them without once looking down or removing his gaze from Jehan's face.

Chasing the boy was like trying to chase lightning. Laurent was using his slimness and freedom from armor to advantage. But Jehan saw the effort it was costing him. Sweat plastered the boy's dark hair against his forehead.

Yet Laurent's determined black gaze hadn't dimmed.

Parrying a new attack, Jehan focused on the fight

while one part of his mind scrambled for a resolution of this tangle to satisfy him, Laurent, and most of all, the woman who watched from the ramparts in unspoken agony. The boy had already earned his pride. Jehan felt more than a grudging admiration for Laurent's hard-learned skills. If it were not for the bloodlust in her brother's eyes, Jehan could imagine he was honing a young squire's talents in the hopes of taking him as one of his men.

Jehan would welcome such a fighter, too, crippled leg and all.

But Laurent would never accept such a position. Not in a house where he thought his sister was treated no better than a whore.

Marry her, screamed his heart, and not for the first time. If the world only knew how much he wanted to slide a ring upon her finger and prove it wasn't just lust that kept him at her side. He defied his prince every day he remained in this castle. He defied a vow of allegiance he'd made before God. He risked the chance that his continual disobedience would destroy the prince's hard-earned favor, leaving Jehan renounced without protection or resources, enemy to English as well as French, as vulnerable as he was when he'd been a penniless man-at-arms turning to thievery on the Gascon hills.

If he married Aliénor, she'd be as vulnerable as he. The thought gutted him just as cold steel bit into his thigh.

By instinct, he took three swift steps back to

restore his stance, grunting as blood stained the wool of his hose. His sword sliced the air as he lifted it in defense. But his move was unnecessary, for the boy had already lost his advantage—one that might have won the match—by freezing in place to stare at the blood seeping through Jehan's hose.

Time to end this.

Jehan moved fast, swinging his sword so hard he forced the boy to angle his weapon in defense as he backtracked, nearly crashing into one of his own men-at-arms before he wheeled off, stumbling. Taking the advantage, Jehan swung the flat of his sword to hit the boy's shoulder and heard Laurent grunt at impact.

Sweat flying from his brow, Jehan turned to see that his sword had grazed Laurent's jaw. Laurent clutch his face, blood running through his fingers, as he took several wobbly steps on his crippled leg before falling to one knee. Jehan surged toward him but his twisting blow to dislodge the sword from Laurent's hand met nothing but air. A slicing sensation seared his upper arm. He jerked away from the sword the boy had maneuvered around his back.

Once again the boy stilled at the sight of blood blossoming, those black eyes going wide. With one sharp kick, Jehan knocked Laurent off the pivot of his knee. The breath came out of him as Laurent sprawled on the ground.

Jehan pointed his sword above the hollow of the boy's throat, where blood pooled from the cut on his jaw.

He shouted, "Yield."

The boy gritted the words, "I will not."

"*Yield.*"

Jehan pressed the tip against the boy's throat. Laurent's sword lay upon the ground, close enough to grab.

"You fought well," Jehan said. "Honor is served."

"Mine perhaps. Not my sister's."

Jehan's nostrils flared. He lifted his gaze to the ramparts. She leaned half over the wall, shaking her head, her hair flying wild.

There could be only one end to this. This boy would accept no conclusion but death—Jehan's or his own.

He held Aliénor's gaze long enough to give the boy courage to move, and the boy did not hesitate to seize the advantage. With the steel of his arm brace, Laurent knocked away the sword pointed at his throat and made Jehan's sword arm fly wide. Jehan loosened his grip so the weapon arced out of his reach. The boy thrust up his own sword while rolling to his feet. The blade clashed against the hem of Jehan's chain-mail shirt. Jehan grunted as it sliced a new wound across the other one on his thigh.

He hardly felt the pain. He faced the boy, pulled his dagger out of its sheath, and deliberately flipped it away so that the knife buried itself to the hilt in the mud beyond his reach.

Then Jehan spread his arms wide.

The boy paused, heaving, his sword raised, confusion rippling across his face.

"I'm unarmed." Jehan flicked his fingers, welcoming him close. "This is what you came for, Laurent de Tournan."

Laurent shifted his weight from his good leg to his bad and then back again. The boy's gaze darted to the ramparts, where his sister watched.

"Ah," Jehan murmured. "So you finally understand."

"Understand *what?*"

"She won't forgive you."

"I'm doing this for *her.*"

"Are you?"

The boy's face darkened. He flexed his elbows and bent his knees, grasping his sword tighter.

"Go ahead." Jehan spread his arms wide. "Go ahead and kill me."

CHAPTER EIGHTEEN

Thibaud held her so tightly he must have expected her to hurl herself bodily over the ramparts. The truth was she was incapable of movement. She'd gone numb right to the marrow of her bones, helpless to do anything but watch the tableau of the mud-trampled field below, where her brother held up a sword against her lover.

A silence fell over the gathered crowd, so heavy it suppressed the creaking of leather, the ring of mail, and the suck of horses' hooves in the mud. Blood pounded in her ears and filled her head with pressure.

This could be a mummer's play, for all that she recognized the two men. Standing there with his arms flung wide, Jehan was the prince's man, the warrior who'd risen to power by the strength of his sword arm, not the man who cradled her in his arms every night. And her little brother now bore no resemblance to the boy who used to curl up in a kitchen cupboard. The man in his place was a sly, wiry fighter whose feints and swift retaliations had drawn blood from a larger, more experienced foe.

Don't kill him.

Her brother stood like a stone, his sword raised.

I love him.

Jehan shifted his gaze to the ramparts and that's how she knew she'd shouted the words. A strange, regretful smile crossed his face. In that smile she saw a thousand kisses, sweet words, warm caresses, the deep peace and satisfaction she felt in the circle of his embrace, the promise of their new life.

But as his smile faded, so did the dreams of the joy they might have had, the life they might have shared, and the family they could have made. Hope drained away like water sluicing out of a tipped water jug.

A curse cut through the silence, shattering the moment. The harsh words she heard fell from her brother's mouth.

With an angry swing of his arm, Laurent tossed his sword away.

Then he fell to one knee in surrender.

***

"Release me, Thibaud."

Aliénor's voice was calm as Jehan led her brother, whose hands were bound before him, into the castle.

Thibaud's grip on her only tightened. "Not now, woman."

"The fight is over."

"Swords are sheathed, but the battle is not settled."

"I will have a say in how it's done."

"This is not woman's work."

"*I* am the woman they fought over," she retorted, as Thibaud's grip caused a painful tingling in her fingers. "Who else is to settle this but me?"

Thibaud's sigh held all the weariness of the world, and when he finally reached the end of it, he let her loose.

Rubbing her upper arms, she strode across the ramparts and stepped into the darkness of the stairs until she reached the bottom. Horses, men-at-arms, pike men, and knights milled in the courtyard. She wove through the crowd until she spotted Jehan dismounting from his horse. Her stomach dropped at the sight of the blood staining his hose and the surcoat below his arm.

She must have made some sound, for he turned and looked directly at her.

She knew every fleck of silver in the depths of those blue eyes. She knew every scar on his skin. She knew the pattern in which black and rust-brown stubble grew upon his jaw, and how his cheeks rounded when he smiled.

But the grim, shuttered face he turned upon her

was that of a stranger.

"That needs tending," she said, gesturing to his leg. "Come inside, I'll see to it—"

"See to your brother first."

The order was like a slap of cold wind. "Your wounds are deeper."

"They look worse than they are. Another woman can tend them."

An argument rose to her lips and would have spilled out if it weren't for the attention they were receiving from the servants and men-at-arms. This conversation, she thought, would be best had in private.

She said, "Where have you put my brother?"

"In the same place your father once put me."

She flinched, remembering the dank, dark, lower room. The expression on her face must have shown her feelings for he turned on a metal heel and strode toward the castle.

Later, she told herself, as she took a deep breath. She could only deal with one irascible, stubborn, foolish man at a time.

She headed toward the kitchens. A cluster of servants muttered in low tones by the door. They raised their heads as she approached, and she was reminded of a herd of deer going still at the crack of a twig in the woods. Except it wasn't fear or wariness she saw in their eyes, but disapproval and a measure of blame.

"Fetch clean linens, wine, and water." She spoke

with all the calm authority she could muster. "And the tallow salve, as well."

They turned their backs and sauntered inside to do her bidding. She felt the heavy pulse of unwelcome. Did she deserve blame? Was this the price to pay for the choices she had made? Would everyone think that, having consorted with Sir Jehan, she'd usurped what rightfully belonged to her own brother? And if her brother truly had renounced the monastery, wasn't that what she'd done, indeed?

A shivering came over her, a kind of unhinging, and to staunch it she focused on practical things. She patted her kirtle pocket and felt the thread and needle she always kept with her. She considered what else she might need to care for Laurent's physical wounds. Soon the cook appeared before her, thin-lipped, thrusting a bowl with linens and unguent in her hands. Hugo loomed out of the darkness behind the servant, carrying water and wine.

With a troubled heart, she led Hugo across the courtyard toward the door leading to Laurent's cell, retracing the same steps she'd once taken, in the dark of night, to tend to Jehan when he had been a prisoner. She felt the stares upon her like a hundred tiny arrow-darts. In all the months she'd lived with Jehan like a wife yet not a wife, she'd never felt even a small portion of such scrutiny she was receiving now. She could hardly breathe for all the attention. It was a relief to pass through the tower door.

When she descended the last turn of the stairs,

she saw two manservants exiting the prison cell and Rudel, the guard, holding the door open for them. Rudel glanced over his shoulder as she arrived. The flickering light cast shadows across his frowning face.

"Sir Rudel," she said, raising the bowl with its linens. "I'm here to tend my brother."

He bowed in grim silence, then gestured for her to enter. The manservants pressed against the wall to make way. Inside, she found the room transformed. Laurent's cell was bright with tallow candles and sconce light. Her brother, wrapped in a fine wool blanket, sat upon a stool next to a table with a goblet of wine.

The man who'd inspired all this attention raised his bloodied face, heaved himself to his feet, and gave her a sad, rueful smile.

"Hello, *sor.*"

She meant to scold him. She intended to rain her frustration upon his mussed, dark head, to call him a reckless fool. But at the sight of him, at the sound of his oh-so-familiar voice, all her intentions crumbled to dust.

She flew across the distance, clattered the bowl upon the table, and threw her arms around him. The scent of blood and pine needles and wood-smoke rose from his clothes. He pressed his head upon her shoulder, just as he used to do as a boy, and it all flashed before her, all those years growing up, stashing him behind barrels to hide him from her father, playing together in the high tower, crying together on the same pallet after they buried their brothers.

She pulled away to look into his face and her heart turned over, for though he'd grown leaner and scruffier, he looked upon her with the same grave, solemn expression she'd always known.

"This is madness," she blurted on a hitch of breath. "You coming here, with an army."

"Courage requires a bit of madness."

"Did some sell-sword tell you that? How thoughtless, Laury, reckless and foolish—"

"Not foolish enough." His nostrils flared. "I couldn't save you."

He pressed his forehead against hers. Words gathered and stuck in her throat. She couldn't deny that amid the tangle of fierce emotions, she felt a glimmer of warmth. But for Jehan, no one had ever tried to save her from anything.

"How," she whispered, swallowing and pulling away from him, "did you ever learn to fight so well?"

"Not easily."

"I'm astonished."

"Because some of Thibaud's teachings finally sank in?"

"Thibaud never taught you how to move so."

He shrugged a shoulder that had gained bulk over the winter. "Sell-swords do have their tricks."

"Does it matter to you I spent every night thinking you'd been murdered?"

"I nearly was." He traced a puckered, badly

knitted scar across his cheekbone. "Twice."

"And why would those men teach you at all?"

"Because I asked them to."

She huffed a sigh. She did not want to have this conversation, so she switched her attention to the slash across his jaw, still bleeding raw.

He touched it gingerly. "It'll leave another scar."

"Yes."

"There go my chances with the fair ladies."

Spoken with a strange grin. In that moment, he was as much a stranger to her as Jehan had seemed, turning his thousand-mile gaze away from her in the courtyard.

She snatched a linen and dunked it in the bowl.

"You look well, Ally."

She wiped the blood from his throat. "Did you expect to find me in ashes and rags?"

"It's some comfort he treats you well."

"He treats everyone well." She dabbed at the edges of the slash. "He treated you well, too, while you were here."

"A pretense. He wanted me gone so he could be alone with you."

That lie had enough truth to bite. "He bought a Bible for you, bound in tooled calfskin, as a gift for Twelfth Night."

"Ironic, to give a Bible to the brother of the woman he dishonored."

"I never once felt dishonored," she retorted, tossing the bloody linen in the bowl of water, "until this very day."

She pulled out her needle and threaded it in thick silence. Laurent turned his head to give her better access. She squeezed the swelling edges together and made the first bloody stitch.

"I didn't mean for that to happen," he said, wincing.

"You didn't mean for it to happen," she mimicked, frustration joining anger as she let the string dangle long enough for her to pat the oozing blood. "What did you expect, when you rode up to this castle to fight for my honor?"

"I told everyone it was to regain my rights as heir."

"Which only complicates everything." She turned her mind away from the difficulties his latest claim would make. "Everyone knew why you were here."

"I know you love him, Ally."

Her throat went as dry as parched fields in a rainless summer.

"But I wonder," he said, his breath hitching at another stitch, "does he love you?"

"Yes."

She spoke the word with confidence though the image flashing through her mind was the distant look on his face as Jehan had dismounted from his horse.

"If he loves you," Laurent said, "then he should have married you."

Her ribs tightened. "He's betrothed to another and bound by a sacred vow."

"His only vow right now is to the prince."

"To whom he owes his loyalty, his livelihood, and his life."

"Then he should have done the honorable thing and sent you away to the king's court—"

"To Paris? On winter roads swarming with thieves?"

"Inconvenience is a very easy excuse."

Laurent's jaw tightened under the split skin now bleeding from multiple puncture wounds. She battled to pat the blood away so she could see what she was doing, though she suspected her sight was impaired as much by tears as by blood.

"I gave myself to him," she blurted. "With a willing heart."

"I know you did."

A flush as hot as flames climbed up her cheeks, a blush she knew the flickering light of the sconces wouldn't hide.

"The shame falls on him, Ally, for letting his ambition rule over love."

"Ambition has nothing to do with it."

"On the contrary. He wanted to have you and whatever fortune the prince is offering to him through a marriage to someone else. In the end, he got both."

Her throat went tight. "I won't listen to this."

"If you refuse to face the truth, then you're no longer the sister I remember."

"You're twisting everything."

She slipped the needle through his skin for the last stitch, pinching off the guilt as he sucked in a breath through his clenched teeth. After cutting the thread, she returned the needle, thread, and scissors to the wool bag in which she stored them.

"I'll bring the Bible Jehan gifted you," she said, gathering the bloodied linens. "Maybe in those pages you'll discover your folly fighting for a woman who does not want to be saved."

"Don't be angry with me, Ally."

"I had a choice." She balled the linens tight in her hands. "I could go to a convent, take a dangerous journey into the court of a stranger, or be wife in all but name to a man I love. So I seized the future I wanted—the one within my reach."

"I had a choice, too," he said, "when I roamed half-starved upon the hills." He stood up so fast that the stool scraped back against the flagstones. "I chose to fight for the honor of my most beloved sister. Would you have me choose otherwise?"

Yes.

No.

Yes.

"Why didn't you do it?" she blurted, her heart pounding. "If you hate Jehan so much, why didn't you kill him?"

"You're wrong on both points."

She shook her head, not understanding.

"I don't hate him, Ally." He hiked his hands to his hips. "And I didn't come here to kill him."

Her head ached trying to make any sense of his words.

"I expected him," he said, "to kill me first."

225

CHAPTER NINETEEN

Jehan sat by a dying fire in the upper room of
the donjon, his armor scattered across the
floor. He thrust his hands through his hair, settled his
elbows on his knees, and bowed his head. He heard
the thick oak door squeal open.

"Get out."

What must he do to let these fools know he
wanted to be alone? He had already thrown out his
squire twice. He wanted no help removing his blood-
splattered doublet, no servant bringing him food or
wine, no better tending to his wound than the linens
he'd tied around his thigh to stop the bleeding. He
wanted to sit in the cold and dark and dirt and blood
and figure out how he could have done everything
differently.

As the door shut, he reimagined the fight on the
field for the hundredth time. What if he had chosen

to make a lightning-swift attack on Laurent's whole contingent instead of allowing a one-on-one challenge? He imagined himself in the thick of that battle, blood pumping hard and battle lust raging in his head, striking at the pike men and the faceless men-at-arms. He imagined, in the midst of the madness, someone striking him from behind, hard enough to drive chain-mail links into his neck. He wouldn't think for long, he would simply react, twisting with his sword high, seeing a cap of dark hair, but not soon enough to deflect his blow or stop the momentum of his swing as it tore through a layer of plated doublet and something else, something soft. In his mind, he watched Laurent claw his chest as Aliénor's scream came from on high.

He clutched his head as that scream shattered inside his skull. Every scenario he imagined ended in Laurent's death or his own—except the one option he'd chosen. Yet mutual survival didn't feel like victory.

The door swung open again. He shot up off the stool with a curse on his lips and then froze in place.

Aliénor stood in the doorway like a stone angel, bathed in the dusky light streaming in through the arrow-slit window. From the very first moment he'd opened his eyes to gaze upon this woman, back in the dimness of his cell, he'd been struck by her beauty. But now, after all their time together, he noticed so much more. His gaze traced the curve of her neck and shoulder but what he remembered was her kindness, her husky laugh, the swift work of her hands, the way she danced back and forth from the buttery, slipped her hand over the backs of her hunting hounds, tossed a fetching look over her shoulder, ran her cool fingers over the fever of his brow.

The air rushed out of his lungs.

She whispered, "It's so cold in here."

He turned away and reached for another log. He set it upon the fire as if the fate of the world hung on how well it balanced upon the crumbling embers.

She said, "Your wounds have not been fully tended."

He shrugged. In his blind fury to be left alone, he'd sent the woman scurrying.

"It's been hours," she said. "Shall I—?"

"No." The word came out harsher than he intended. "The wounds aren't deep." He planted a hand on the mantel and forced his voice calm. "How is your brother?"

"Changed."

The word was spoken with such ruefulness that he hazarded a glance at her. She stood with a knot between her brows, stroking the clean linens hanging over her forearm. Her steady calm unnerved him more than weeping. He *wished* she would weep, wail aloud, or strike him with fists and angry words.

He deserved that.

He said, "You've come to plead his case?"

"No."

He raised a brow.

"He will speak his own mind," she said. "Laurent will not pay a moment's mind to what I advise, I assure you."

Frustration surged in him. She *had* to know what he must do now, as the protector of this castle. Her brother had marched here with an army, calling himself the one true heir. If Jehan didn't act swiftly to stanch that claim, the question as to who ruled would linger. The villagers might choose the boy they knew, taking up arms against Jehan as the holder of the prince's claim. If Jehan didn't act, he'd be leaving himself and all who depended upon him vulnerable to conflict.

"You won't kill him," she said softly. "You had a chance, and you didn't."

He turned his face away from her.

"You won't kill him," she repeated, "because you love me."

A knight wore layers of armor to avoid injury. A padded doublet beneath a shirt of mail, pounded metal buckled to his elbows, his forearms, his calves, and molded to his feet. But a heart had no armor, and no weapon had ever plunged deeper than her words.

He turned away from her and allowed himself to imagine another scenario. He saw sunlight shining on her golden hair, crowned with flowers, as they stood together outside the door of the chapel. He saw Father Dubose wrapping a cloth around their clasped hands. He imagined villagers gathering in a cluster around them, crying out as the final words were spoken and the blessing placed upon them. He dreamed of Aliénor's bright, wide smile as she lifted her face for the marriage kiss.

Then still another scenario rushed through the scene like a storm. The clatter and roar of a hundred men-at-arms gathered outside the castle, striking their swords against their shields. Perhaps they were English, detouring from the next scouring of Gascony to fetch Jehan back to Bordeaux to be executed, his lands and castle and unsanctioned wife taken away. Or perhaps they were French knights, arriving in force to win back what was stolen, now that the knight who held it had fallen so out of favor with the Prince of Wales that the English would no longer raise a finger in defense.

He shook the images from his head. Swiveling on a foot, he crossed the short distance separating them and took her face between the palms of his hands. Her cheeks were flushed but cold. He held them until they grew warm from his touch.

"I do love you," he said, his voice gruff.

Her mouth trembled. He remembered too well how it felt pillowed under his own.

He added, "I think I've loved you from the first moment I laid eyes upon you."

"That's not true." Her voice, husky and low. "You were all but dead then."

"You brought my body back to life," he said. "And my heart."

She grasped his hands, flexing her own over his, but he couldn't allow hope to bloom so he tightened his grip. "I have to send you away, Aliénor."

"I know."

She didn't know. She couldn't possibly. But her steady gaze, growing misty with tears, proved him wrong.

"Everything has changed," she whispered, with a hitch in her throat. "I feel it in the way everyone looks at me, or avoids looking at me. I don't understand why, not completely, except Laurent's foolish actions are the cause of it. If I stayed, I'd be making a mockery of him and of what the world would consider good and…"

"Honorable," he said, whispering the word she could not.

"Yes," she conceded. "If I stayed," she continued, working her way through what he'd known the moment Laurent had brought a small army to the gates, "then *I'd* be the enemy. I'd be the traitor choosing an English conqueror, even in the face of my brother's claim. They'd take up his cause, Jehan. They'd turn against us. *All* of them."

He leaned forward and pressed his lips against her forehead, breathing in the scent of spring in her hair. She had always been like this, willing to face even the hardest truths.

Then her fingers crept up to cup his jaw, forcing him to look at her, to see what she wanted him to see. Those expressive eyes filled with emotion as her body softened against his.

He could no more resist that oh-so-familiar invitation than he could stop his heart from beating. He plunged one hand into her thick hair and captured her mouth with his. He tried to get closer, ever closer, until the cold stones of the wall scraped the back of his hand. Everything was movement and moans, the tug of cloth and jangle of buckles, captured breath and sudden gasps, no moment to think of anything but the blinding hunger between them, the sore pounding of his heart, the hollow of his hands aching for the feel of her until finally, *finally*, the weight of a breast filled his palm.

She made those sweet little noises in the back of her throat. His cock hardened, pressing against his loosened linens, throbbing. Setting his member free to press against her thigh, he shifted his grip to burrow his other hand between them, probing through folds of linen as she widened her stance for his touch, until he felt the wet welcome of her.

With a groan he lifted her up by the buttocks so she could straddle his hips. He yanked cloth aside so his cock, tight and hard, would find its home. To the music of her gasp, she sheathed him like a sword. He pulled back and plunged deeper, and then did it again, feeling her hot insides gripping him. He wanted to penetrate much more than her body as they found a rhythm. He wanted to leave his imprint on her so she wouldn't forget what they had, wouldn't forget *him*.

Because, in his heart, he knew this lovemaking

would change nothing. They would still have to part. He felt her desperation as strongly as he felt his own. This would be the last time he would taste the skin of her throat, smell the wind in her hair, or feel her fists gripping his shoulders as her body closed ever more tightly around him.

Her inner muscles throbbed as she threw her head back with a cry. She convulsed against him in a pleasure he made more intense by reaching between them to circle with a fingertip the most sensitive part of her. He would make her shudder again before he took his own measure of release, if only to look upon the lovely face he'd made soft with desire grow even more flushed with the pleasure he could give her.

He shifted his position, continuing to thrust—short, shallow little thrusts, so he could continue to slide his fingertip along the folds of her cleft, spreading the moisture of her sex around the root of his cock and across the nub of her pleasure. He breathed hard against the rise of her breast as she threaded her fingers through his hair. Their eyes met and held and he never wanted to look away.

"Aliénor," he gasped, as her inner muscles clenched him hard.

She called out his name—a cry of surprise as a wave stronger than before shuddered through her body. Feeling her succumb again threatened to destroy the last shred of his control. He held back a single moment longer, long enough to pull himself out of her before he spilled his seed.

He couldn't restore her innocence—that he'd taken, a thief still—but he could protect her this way, at least.

He stood for a long time, pressing her body against the wall with her thighs wrapped around his waist, while they both breathed hard. He held her until he could no longer bear the burning of the wound on his thigh. By degrees, he released her, feeling every curve of her body as she slid to her feet. Holding her languid gaze, he finally peeled their bodies apart.

Cold air rushed between them. She leaned back against the wall, her hair disheveled, the neckline of her kirtle askew, her bunched skirts slipping down. She was so seductive and beautiful and strong and *his*. With a soft smile, she straightened the cloth of her kirtle. He rearranged his clothing as well, retreating to the hearth as if to give her privacy, but really so he wouldn't continue to stare at her as if she were water and he a man dying of thirst.

"Wherever you want to go," he murmured, casting a glance over his shoulder to soften his words, "I'll see it done, Aliénor."

Fussing to fix the neckline of her kirtle, she nodded. "Tomorrow, I'll leave for Paris."

Her gentle determination cut a new wound in his heart. King Jean, his court, and maybe her father were in Paris. A Gascon heiress, even a dispossessed one, could be married off to some ambitious knight in the hope that the French king would help the groom recapture his new wife's lost inheritance.

Every time he cast his thoughts to the future, he saw Aliénor standing by another man's side.

He tightened his jaw as he laid a steadying hand on the mantel. "I will escort you."

"No, no," she said, arranging her skirt straight across her hips. "It's too deep into French territory."

"I will not send you unguarded."

"Thibaud would be a better escort, along with some of my father's remaining men-at-arms."

"With no offense to your uncle, he's not the spryest knight in this castle."

"But he has influence in the French court, if his stories are to be believed."

"In the court of the king's father, perhaps, but–"

"Jehan, certainly you understand it would better that I arrive in Paris with my uncle rather than my lover."

"Then I shall leave you at the gates."

A blush glazed her cheeks. He could see it from clear across the room. She was ashamed, he thought. Laurent and his grand, reckless, thoughtless gesture had made her ashamed of what they had shared between them.

That might be the worst wound of all.

"And my brother," she ventured, clasping her hands before her. "What are you to do with him?"

Indeed, what was he to do with the brother who'd convinced brigands to fight for his cause? A boy who'd ridden to this castle in the colors of his father and fought for his sister's honor? A crippled boy warrior who claimed to be heir?

"Go and tell your brother," he said, "that I will send you away to your king—but only under the condition that he join the monastery and publicly cede his claim to the title for good."

"You know he has never wanted the title."

"Yet just by making the claim, he may have started something he can no longer control."

She raised her shoulders in frustration. "He's so changed, Jehan. I can't promise he'll concede."

"He'll concede because it's what he truly wants. He can accompany us, to see the bargain complete."

She looked overlong at her clasped hands, the silence broken only by the crackling of the hearth flames.

"I can't help but wonder," she ventured. "Wouldn't it be…unwise…for us to travel so long and far together?"

His heart constricted. Already he longed to run kisses along the side of her face to where a pulse now beat against her temple.

"Not with your brother and uncle as chaperones," he said. "I can escort Laurent to the monastery on the return journey."

She nodded in silence, her chest rising and falling, her throat flexing, her gaze slipping away from his.

"I can't leave him here in my absence, in any case," he added, "for sell-swords or the villagers to rally to his misguided cause. Now go." It hurt to look at her so he turned to gaze sightlessly at the fire. "Make your brother the offer, and then make the arrangements for the journey. We leave tomorrow."

A bird flew close to the arrow-slit, coming up against the barrier of the stretched leather covering. The sound of battering wings filled the room. By the time the noise stopped, Aliénor had already slipped out the door.

He laid his head upon his hand where it gripped the mantle.

The fight was over.

Her brother had won.

CHAPTER TWENTY

Sunlight flashed on Jehan's arm brace as he lifted his hand to signal a halt.

Because Aliénor spent every day of their weary voyage with her gaze fixed on the small column of riders that led to Paris—with Jehan always at its head—she was the first to pull her horse to a stop.

She watched as her former lover bent closer to a man-at-arms, exposing a stretch of his bare neck. Since leaving Castelnau over three weeks ago, Jehan had worn limited armor so as not to wear out the horses. Although she understood the need for speed through the war-pitted country, she couldn't help but notice how vulnerable the curve of his neck looked without a chain mail coif to protect it.

With a pang, she pushed the thought away and spoke to Thibaud and her brother, riding on either side. "Brigands, do you think?"

"I doubt it," her brother said. "This is open countryside."

"But for that copse up ahead," Thibaud grunted. "Perfect for an ambush on a merchant's caravan this close to Paris. I'll go see what's what."

Her stomach did a sloping drop, less for the risk of an ambush and more for the sound of the words *close to Paris*. As soon as Thibaud nudged his horse ahead, she asked Laurent, "How far?"

"To the copse? Not more than a few—"

"Don't play the fool, Laury. How far to Paris?"

He paused a moment too long. "I don't know."

"You're a terrible liar."

She knew he lied because whenever they camped in the open under the stars in some secluded place, she would curl by a fire and watch Jehan from beneath her lashes as he talked to Laurent and the others about the routes they would take and the distances they would make, in voices almost too low for her to hear.

"It wasn't so long ago," Laurent said, "when you forbade me to even speak the name of the city we are going to."

"Paris was very far away then."

"It has been a hard journey. Surely you want it to end?"

"I don't mind the travel."

"It isn't the travel of which I speak."

She worried the leather of the reins between her fingers. With Thibaud always snoring on one side of the fire and her brother muttering in his sleep on the other, she was, essentially, without chaperones. But whenever she rose up in the darkness on the excuse of privacy, Jehan did not slip away from the other fire to follow her. Whenever she kicked her mount hoping to talk with him on the road, he ordered her back to where she'd be surrounded by her uncle, brother, and the four men-at-arms. Jehan was sparing with his gaze, except when he came upon her washing by a river, or when he brushed past her in the crowded hall of an inn. She lived to see that flare of wanting in his eyes, a glimpse of the lover he hid all too quickly.

Soon, she would never see it again.

"I'll miss you, *sor*."

Her brother's words drew her from her thoughts. Jehan would not be the only one she would leave behind when she stepped through Parisian gates, though at times she felt like Laurent's long winter in the hills had already stolen away the boy she'd once known.

"I will see you again," she said. "You will visit Paris when you're a monk. You will have to see the bishop, go on pilgrimages, and make the rounds of the churches."

Laurent grunted and found something of interest on the far horizon.

This was not the first time her brother had slipped into silence at the mention of his future. "Laury," she said. "You made a promise to Jehan."

"Sir Jehan's offer was generous beyond reason."

"Then why do you get broody whenever I bring it up?"

"I don't want to have this conversation with you."

"You never do."

"I ask you to be respectful of my wishes."

"I would, if time weren't running out."

"Ally…" She could see by the deepening ripples on his forehead he was thinking hard. "Things have changed." His shoulders rose and fell. "*I* have changed."

"I've noticed."

She no longer jolted with surprise seeing how straight he sat his horse or with what ease he wore the dagger, baldric, and sword. On the contrary, she made a point of trying *not* to notice such things. Those changes needled her because of the part they played in bringing her here, only miles from the gates of Paris, soon to say good-bye to Jehan forever.

"I've given up all my claims as heir," he said with a careless shrug. "You always deserved that over me anyway. But the monastery…"

"What?"

"It feels like an old dream. Someone else's dream."

"It was yours once, and you wanted nothing more than a life of prayer and fasting and celibacy."

A flush made his throat as blotchy as if he'd come down with a spotted disease, and then she was sure of it: There *had* been a woman during that winter in the hills.

"Someday," she said with a raised brow, "you'll have to tell me all the details about your winter travels."

"It doesn't matter." He gripped the pommel of his saddle as tightly as he'd held those secrets from her, despite all her prying. "Since I have no real choice in this matter, the monastery it is. *Fini.* But I do have a confession for you."

She perked up.

"You were right," he said, "all along."

"Music to my ears," she said. "But about what?"

"About Sir Jehan." Laurent glanced forward to where Jehan still talked in a low voice to Thibaud and a man-at-arms. "He's an honorable man, in the end."

"Of course he is." Laurent's belated respect only tightened the knot in her belly, but she forced herself not to hold anger close. If she dwelt too long on Laurent's part in this separation, she would grow to resent him. "You should have taken me at my word."

He squinted up at the cloudless sky. "Hard riding under an open sky makes for strange bedfellows and unexpected alliances," he said, "but it wouldn't have changed a single thing I did."

"Of course not," she said tightly. "I don't want to talk about this."

"You never do."

"Respect my wishes, Laury."

"I would, if time weren't running out—"

"Look," she interrupted, kicking her horse forward. "Thibaud is checking the hooves of Jehan's horse."

"You're not getting off so easily." The leather of his saddle creaked as her brother kept pace. "There's proof you're more stubborn than I."

"Jehan's horse must have thrown a shoe, don't you think?"

"I know he loves you, Ally."

The air rushed out of her.

"If he had married you, I would have been proud to call him my brother."

Then the clatter of hooves brought her attention back to Jehan, upon his horse, riding bold and hard toward them.

"Don't reach for your swords," Jehan said in a low voice, yanking his horse to a stop. "Men up ahead. A dozen maybe."

He spoke to the men-at-arms behind her, avoiding her gaze.

"We'll ride ahead on the road as if we don't see them," Jehan said. "Upon my signal, we'll spread out and gallop in through the trees, flanking them."

Then that blue gaze strayed to her and every inch of her body came alive. "My lady, stay upon the path at some distance behind." His gaze shifted to her brother. "Laurent, we're outnumbered, so we could use your sword."

Beside her, Laurent nodded.

Jehan pulled his horse around to lead the group

forward. The men sipped from their leather water bladders and discreetly adjusted the sag of their baldrics. The last time they had all run into a skirmish, they'd come around a curve to find a merchant's cart turned over in the mud. But the brigand's road block hadn't been enough to overcome the well-trained, well-armed, mounted knights around her. Still, the shouts, grunts, and clashing of swords had been unnerving, reminding her of the terrible day when the English flooded over the ramparts of Castelnau.

The path to the copse was rutted by thousands of cart wheel tracks and scattered with tufts of grass. The horses must have sensed the tension for her mare tugged at the bit as they were forced into a steady pace, keeping up the illusion that they did not know of the would-be attackers hidden in the trees.

Responding to some subtle signal, the men-at-arms kicked their horses and passed her on either side to fan out toward the trees. Laurent bent over the neck of his horse and slipped into alignment next to Thibaud as if he'd practiced the move all his life. She held her horse steady amid the tumult, dropping back from the men. As Jehan entered the shadows, she heard the first clash of steel on steel.

She pulled her horse to a stop and stood in uneasy solitude while the wind coming over the field pressed her skirts against her horse's side. Her breath sounded loud in her own ears so she held it so she could better listen to what was happening. Between the trees, she could see the occasional flash of sword, a blur of pale surcoat, the flick of horses' hooves. Men shouted orders and she couldn't tell one voice from another—only Jehan's, deep and harsh.

All of a sudden a man and a horse wheeled out of the copse onto open ground and she recognized the rider. Her brother swung a sword against a knight on foot. Laury worked the reins with one hand while he wielded a sword with the other. On horseback, his crippled foot was no hindrance at all.

As her throat tightened with every swing, a pair of men shot out from the line of trees, driven by another mounted man. Aliénor thought she'd never want to see Jehan and Laurent fighting on the same field again, but here they fought as allies. She listened to the grunts and shouts, and watched one and then the other as they fended off the attack and worked their enemies weary. They protected each other's backs, until the enemy fighters realized they were outmatched and darted back into the wood.

The ringing of swords and the shouts ebbed to a restless silence. Thibaud broke through the trees to join Jehan and Laurent, followed by the men-at-arms.

Thibaud rode to her side. "They were a raggedy group of sell-swords, claiming they worked for King Jean." Thibaud pulled off his helmet and his white hair sprang free. "They said they were keeping an eye out for the approach of the English army, but I'm not sure—"

"They'll return, whoever they are," Jehan said, joining them. "They know the strength of our forces so they'll bring three times as many to offset us."

Thibaud said, "We could take the river road instead—"

"The king's sword-hires are watching the waterways for sure." Jehan turned his horse in a circle, eyeballing the countryside, his gaze lingering on the west. "It's time for English and French to go our own ways."

Her heart dropped.

"Thibaud," Jehan said, "I leave it to you and your two men-at-arms to bring your great-niece to Paris."

"We passed a monastery a few miles back," Thibaud said, musing. "There'll be other travelers there."

"Go back, then," Jehan said, "and join them for protection for the last day's journey."

Last day's journey.

"No," she said, in a whisper. "Not yet."

Jehan ignored her, his jaw tightening, as he turned to her brother. "My men-at-arms will accompany you to the monastery in Toulouse, Laurent."

Laurent nodded and then kicked his horse beside hers. "Farewell for now, *sor.*"

His hand left her grip before she realized he'd grasped it. Laurent turned his horse away, his expression, beneath a wispy excuse of a mustache, full of regret. Everyone was moving again, men and horses separating into groups. She pulled the reins tight as if by stilling her horse she could stop all this, only to find Jehan looming before her, sitting straight and tall on his restless war horse.

She fell into his blue eyes. For the first time since they'd last embraced she saw the ache, the torment, and the regret in them. She felt an overwhelming urge to reach out, to feel the strength of his arms around her and the warmth of his lips on her brow, one more memory to add to the others.

But he sat his horse too far away and held his feelings too close.

"Where will you go?" she whispered, her head spinning, her heart in her throat. "Unprotected, alone, in French territory?"

"I'll find my liege lord, the prince," he said. "Rumor has it he's driving his army toward Poitiers."

She searched for her own future in those eyes but it was no longer there. Soon he would have a new wife, an English wife. His wife would be rich and young and bear him children who would continue his name. She might have a new husband, too, given to her by the king of France. Her marriage would bring her security, perhaps affection, at best mutual respect.

But never the kind of love she'd experienced with Jehan.

She was caught in his gaze like a sparrow in a whirlwind.

Her heart murmured, *I love you, I love you, I love you.*

And then he was gone.

CHAPTER TWENTY-ONE

Palais de la Cité, Paris

"*Aliénor de Tournan.*"

The words echoed in the rafters of the royal palace. She stilled among the row of stone pillars carved with the likenesses of the kings of France, sure she'd dreamt what she'd just heard.

"Thibaud," she blurted, gripping his arm.

"*Aliénor de Tournan, come forward before your prince.*"

Her uncle moved into action, shoving a shoulder between two clergymen standing in front of them before thrusting her bodily into the gap. When the strangers whirled in outrage, she slipped around them only to crash into others.

"Coming through," Thibaud bellowed, elbowing deeper into the great hall. "His Grace the Dauphin has summoned my kinswoman. *Let. Us. Through.*"

Though she'd been living in Paris for months, Aliénor still couldn't believe the crush of petitioners who swarmed every official court gathering. King Jean wasn't even in residence—either then or now. He'd marched his army south to stop the approach of the Prince of Wales' forces. He'd left behind his hapless and powerless representatives to hear the pleas of the dispossessed from a war that had made beggars of them all. And now King Jean was a prisoner of the English, captured during the disastrous battle at Poitiers.

With so much upheaval, she'd all but given up ever having her petition for aid and succor heard. Yet now, as she stumbled into the clearing before the dais, she found herself face-to-face with the king's firstborn son Charles, the Dauphin and acting regent of France.

She dipped into a curtsey beside a bowing Thibaud, very glad she'd made the effort to fix a tear on the hem of her honey-colored kirtle last night.

A low, bored voice spoke her name.

"Yes." She straightened up. "Yes, it is I, Your Grace."

The regent, red-headed, ruddy-faced, and perhaps a few years younger than herself, sprawled in a carved, gilded chair pushed away from a black marble table. Unsurprisingly, he looked weary. He'd returned from a crushing military defeat to take his seat in a bankrupt city, with the people in revolt, and a French contender for his father's throne churning up discontent all through the countryside.

The regent tapped the desk upon which was spread a wealth of parchments. "It says here you're from Gascony."

"Yes, Your Grace." She swallowed the lump in her throat to deliver the one piece of news that had found its way to their humble lodgings near the Abbey of St. Martin. "My father, the Viscount of Tournan, fought beside your father at Poitiers. My father died on the field of battle."

She lowered her head not to hide raw grief, but a lingering sorrow. In truth, she'd lost her father years ago at Crécy.

"Many a good man died on the battlefield," the regent said, nodding his head, as she'd seen him do many times when other petitioners spoke similar words. "My sympathies, mademoiselle, for your loss."

"Thank you, Your Grace."

"Your father's lands," he said, as he ran his fingers over the three stripes of ermine on the sleeve of his robe. "Where are they?"

"On the border between Aquitaine and the lands of the counts of Toulouse," she said, as Thibaud had tutored her, "at least the border as it once stood before the prince burned his way across Gascony."

The regent leaned to one side and perused a map one of his aides had lifted into the light. Beside her, Thibaud shifted his weight, stifled by the protocol forbidding him from addressing the regent before being spoken to.

Lifting his gaze from the map, the regent asked, "How many castles?"

"One castle seat." By the way the regent's lips tightened, he clearly thought a single castle a meager estate. "We had another," she added, "but the English took it earlier in the war—"

"One castle," he interrupted, "and another one stolen, and yet you have friends in high places."

"Your Grace?"

"I've received not one but *two* petitions in your name, mademoiselle."

She sidled her uncle a confused glance. His face was turning red with the effort to hold his tongue. "Perhaps my uncle," she ventured, "who has some history in your grandfather's service, can clarify—"

"I have read your uncle's petition. It's the *other* that intrigues me." He lifted a paper from one of the piles. Light sifted through it so she could see a dark wax seal weighing it down. "This one arrived just yesterday," he said. "It's written by a knight in the Prince of Wales' service."

A tingling passed over her skin, like a thousand little pinpricks piercing her from scalp to toes.

"The knight writes quite eloquently for a traitorous Gascon," the regent continued, tilting the paper to the light. "*...the lady, as my chatelaine, held the castle for her family and kept its people safe long beyond what should be possible in a country ravaged by plague, famine, and war, showing strength of character and loyalty to King Jean that wins high praise even from those whom she calls her enemies...*"

She couldn't seem to catch her breath.

Not dead by a French scout's sword.

Not dead by a brigand's dagger.

Not dead on the field of battle.

She bathed in Jehan's words while white light streamed from the high windows and poured across the paving stones at her feet.

"I assume you know this knight, mademoiselle?" The paper rustled in the regent's hand. "This…St. Simon?"

I know the way the corner of his lips tilt when he's amused, the way his lids grow heavy as he looks upon me, the way he stands with his shoulders sloped when he's in thought, planning something, thinking of a future I can never share.

She stuttered, "I do, Your Grace."

The regent's voice, thick with impatience. "Well?"

"Sir Jehan is the English knight," she said, daring to speak his name for the first time in months, "who seized both of my castles."

The ripples of the regent's forehead pressed up against the rim of his crown. "A Gascon knight with English loyalties speaking in support of the very heiress he dispossessed?"

She lowered her head to find her hands clasped in a grip of prayer. "Apparently so, Your Grace."

"Why?" he barked. "Why would an English knight plead a French noblewoman's cause, when it can benefit him none and cause him no end of trouble should you rally a French knight to take up your banner?"

Because he loves me and I love him and the whole world conspires to keep us apart.

She said, "This will take some explaining."

"My lady, these days three things elude me: Good news, good wishes, and good stories." He tossed the paper on the table and waved at her. "Proceed at will."

She smoothed her hands down her skirts, biding for time as she marshalled her scattered thoughts. The truth was a better story than the tale Thibaud had concocted for her, but Thibaud had forbidden her to speak the truth to anyone. She'd only agreed because her great-uncle had warned that the regent would likely toss her into a convent if it was made known she'd taken an English lover.

So, as dispassionately as she could, she recited the events leading up to the loss of her castle and her decision, after the dark winter of the Prince's raids, to seek the protection of her father's liege lord. She told the tale without ever mentioning she'd spent the cold winter snug and happy in Jehan's bed.

As she finished, the regent said into the silence, "This is a weary, common tale—"

"If I may be so bold, Your Grace." Thibaud interrupted, stepping forward to fall on one knee.

The regent raised pale brows at her great-uncle's breach of protocol, but waved away the guard who'd stepped forward. "Thibaud de Pirou, I presume?"

"At your service."

"Your niece said earlier you knew my grandfather."

"I fought for King Philip VI at both Crécy and Calais."

"Ah." The regent leaned forward. "My grandfather was full of stories."

"I know of exploits that I wager not even *you* have been told."

The regent's grin was quick and surprisingly boyish. "You must tell me every one. All I hear in these terrible days are of burning and plundering and rebellion."

"With your permission, I'll tell you a tale now, one that will lift your spirits. It involves the young brother of the lady who stands before you."

The regent's smile dimmed. "She has a brother?"

"A crippled one," Thibaud said. "Long disowned by his father—"

"But yet still living."

"Bound by honor to join a monastery," Thibaud added, "and no threat to the claims of his sister. Yet this boy was the agent of a great victory—"

"Impossible." The regent cut a glance to one of the knights behind the throne. "I'm told victories no longer occur in France."

"This was a victory not of war but of honor." Thibaud stood up from his kneel. "If you but give me a moment of your time, Your Grace, I shall tell a tale of valor and virtue unlike any you've ever heard."

***

"Come sit with me, Blanche." Aliénor slid onto a bench at the far end of the great hall in the castle outside Meaux, a little town about twenty-five miles northeast of Paris. "If we're talking together, maybe all these courtiers will leave us alone."

"My dear," the woman said, adjusting her voluminous skirts as she sat on the bench beside her, "no man in the room is likely to leave *you* alone."

"Flatterer."

"But I'll sit with you anyway, in the hopes of catching a leftover."

"Blanche, stop. You deserve better than a 'leftover.'"

"Duckling, we *are* the leftovers, remember?"

Aliénor pulled a face at her friend. She'd met this forty-year-old, irrepressible widow on the first night she and Thibaud had dined at court, when they were seated together far, far below the salt. The court swarmed with the dispossessed, eating freely of the regent's generous bounty, and she and Blanche were only two ladies out of hundreds now under the regent's care.

"Ah," Blanche said, with a sudden edge in her voice. "Look there. Your great-uncle is making a fool of himself again."

Aliénor turned her attention to the blur of dancing. Thibaud was among the dancers, his back military-straight, saying something to make his partner laugh. Aliénor marveled at her kinsman. For a man who'd spent most of his time pacing the ramparts of Castelnau and sparring on the training field, he moved among these ladies and courtiers as if he'd been born with royal blood. In the weeks since they'd joined the French court, Thibaud had spun gold out of his dusty old stories and made more friends than she could keep up with.

"That uncle of yours," Blanche continued, "should spend less time dancing and more time seeing to your welfare."

"He would say he's doing just that, making influential friends and connections." For reasons Aliénor didn't quite understand, Thibaud and the widow had been at odds since they'd met. "In any case, right now he's far too busy with the regent to worry about matchmaking."

And that's just fine by me.

"Your uncle is doing nothing but spinning fanciful yarns for the regent's pleasure. I wouldn't be surprised if he took the fool Mitton's place in the regent's affections."

"Blanche, please, he's my kinsman."

"All the more reason why he should see you settled. Thibaud's not getting any younger, and neither are you."

"So quick to marry me off, are you?"

"What's the alternative, my dear? Staying here, suffering a lifetime of listening to the whining of the regent's wife?"

"Have pity on the duchess, she's hugely

pregnant."

"And she makes sure we all remember it every time she's loaded into another carriage and the entire court is dragged to yet another provincial castle on the regent's whim."

Hardly on the regent's whim, but Aliénor didn't want to argue the point. She wouldn't soon forget the day last month when an angry mob of peasants had broken into the royal palace in Paris and killed two marshals right before the regent's eyes. Since then, the whole court had been traveling from fortress to fortress in a wide circle around Paris so the young regent could fortify them before returning to take the rebellious city by storm.

The city of Paris, it seemed, was as unsettled as her own heart.

"Pardon my interruption," came a voice from above, "but do I have the honor of speaking to Aliénor de Tournan?"

The words were polite and courtly but it was the Gascon accent that slipped beneath her defenses. The slide of the man's vowels raised memories of the bright silver ribbon of the Arrats, the warmth of the rock slope beneath her feet, the scent of ripe grapes on the autumn wind, the ducks waddling in the muddy courtyard. She glanced up, hope rising for a familiar face, but the man was a tall, young stranger who looped a thumb under his low-slung baldric as he gazed upon her with deference.

Aliénor said. "Are we acquainted, sir?"

"We have never met," he said, with a bow, "but the regent just informed me of your presence. I am newly returned from Gascony on orders to report about the strongholds no longer in our hands."

She sucked in a breath. "You saw Castelnau?"

"Yes." A sad smile flittered across his face. "Though it is thinly guarded, mademoiselle, it is still in English hands."

"And St. Simon," she said, trying hard not to stutter over the name, "is he still in possession?"

"His colors flew from the ramparts, indeed, but he was not in attendance."

"Oh?"

She held this young man's gaze like a straw that would keep her from drowning. She hated how desperate she sounded, but the rumors and gossip flooding the court rarely included any news about English knights. She was desperate for information.

"He's in London." The young man watched her face with great care. "With the prince himself, so the villagers of Castelnau told me."

She swallowed and nodded while her thoughts vaulted to Jehan in England, perhaps meeting his new bride.

"And…the village," she added, deflecting, "and my people?"

"The villagers were out in the fields when I arrived, harvesting a fine crop. It was a rare sight, one of the few pleasing ones I saw. Most villages and bastides in the area were burnt to the ground, their fields destroyed."

She bobbed her head, words failing her.

"If I may be so bold, mademoiselle…"

"Yes?"

"Is it true you remained in the castle after St. Simon captured it?"

"Yes."

"Then I commend you for your bravery and loyalty."

"Bravery?" She seized the end of her tippet, running it through her fingers until it crackled in the dry air. "It's not bravery to stay safe within my own home while war rages beyond the walls."

"I speak of your refusal to become the English knight's bride."

Her fingers stilled on the tippet. Beside her, Blanche shifted on the bench. Her gown rustled like dry leaves.

"Sir," Aliénor said, speaking through a tight throat. "Sir Jehan made me no such offer."

"You jest."

"He was all but married," she retorted, wanting a quick end to this conversation. "The Prince of Wales promised him to an English lady."

"Ah, a prince's promise would be hard for an ambitious man to resist."

The shame falls on him, Laurent had once said, *for letting ambition rule over love.*

"Still," the knight added, "a man is generally better served securing what he holds in his hands rather than hoping for something that might never come to pass. From what I know of St. Simon, I'd have expected him to seize what he could."

God's Blood, she couldn't help herself. "You know him, sir?"

"In passing." His attention drifted to the swirl of dancers in the room. "Sir Jehan and I have met on more than one occasion, which is one reason why your particular situation has attracted my interest."

Heat crept up from the neckline of her kirtle. She'd done her best to deflect suspicion of what had really happened over winter, but this man now had her wondering if he knew more than he should. He was dressed in a close-fitting tunic with dagged edges, all the style in the French court. The flicker of the rush lights shone on the gold threads in his doublet, yet in the shadows she couldn't make out the colors.

He certainly wore finer clothing than any simple messenger, which is what she'd first assumed him to be.

"You are upsetting my friend, sir," Blanche said, bless her, as the widow covered Aliénor's hand with her own. "Her losses are great."

The man's attention returned to them swiftly. "My apologies, ladies, I forget myself." He put his feet together and offered a bow. "Mademoiselle Aliénor, I'd hoped to introduce myself if the opportunity ever arose, for our families have a connection."

When he straightened up, light rippled over his

doublet and she caught sight of his heraldry at last.

"Guy de Baste, at your service," he said, as a smile curved his lips. "I believe we were once nearly betrothed."

CHAPTER TWENTY-TWO

Aliénor stared out the leaded windows onto the sun-drenched field with the longing of a drunkard for a goblet of wine.

"Come, Blanche," she said, knowing she sounded like a long-denied child, "let's quit this stuffy room and walk through the fields."

"Have you lost your senses?" Blanche raised her gaze from her embroidery. "It's hot enough out there to bake a hen in its nest."

"In Gascony, the heat of the summer is far worse than this."

"Well, first, I am not Gascon. And second—"

"How can you breathe in this room?" Tossing her embroidery in the basket, she stood up from her chair so abruptly that it clattered. "I swear I shall suffocate if I don't get some air."

Ignoring the starts, stares, and raised brows of

the other ladies, including the heavily pregnant regent's wife, Aliénor headed out of the solar. She was tired of being cooped up like the sparrow hawk she'd left behind in Castelnau under Sir Rostand's care. Most of all, she was tired of listening to what she *should* do, what she *must* do, what she was *expected* to do. If the world conspired to order her life, then she would take freedom in any small way she could.

So she bounded down the stairs to the great hall. In the vaulted room, courtiers, supplicants, and men-at-arms mingled, enjoying wine while dogs turned and turned in tight circles, seeking the coolest stones in the shadowed corners. She ignored the curious looks cast her way, ducking her head so as not to catch any man's eye, and followed a straight and unwavering path to the front door of the castle.

She was out the door long before Blanche followed her with a wobbling, worried shout of her name.

"We shouldn't be here," Blanche sputtered as she caught up with her. "None of us should be outside today."

Aliénor frowned at the iron portcullis, lowered to block access to the cool green fields beyond the castle gates. "This is foolishness."

"It's for our protection," Blanche insisted. "You know that horrid man, the mayor of Meaux, has been allowing armed peasants into the city."

"Rumors, nothing more."

"Rumor or not, do you want to be trapped in an

open field when vicious men attack this castle?"

"Blanche, there's a river between us and the village."

"And a bridge they can cross—"

"—which is as narrow as it can be. From these ramparts, the regent's archers can pick off any attackers, one at a time."

"Oh, please, Aliénor, I can't bear it when you speak so." She clasped her hands over her wimple. "If the men believe we're in danger, then we should listen and stay inside."

Aliénor exhaled in frustration. The regent was frequently away from his court, dispersing riots, testing the strength of the Parisian defenses, and seeking to confront the pretender Navarre wherever he could. He'd long confined all those who remained here to stay on the island and not venture over the bridge into the village. Today, it seemed, the circle of forbidden travel had shrunk to within the fortress walls looming around her.

If only she could turn herself into a sparrow hawk and soar over them! Maybe if she flew high and far enough, she could see the view from Castelnau, the rolling fields unfurling to the horizon, the darkness of the forest to the west, the wild places she could lose herself in whenever worries wore her down.

"You, my dear, are in such a state as I've never seen you." Blanche slipped her arm through Aliénor's and tugged her into a stroll around the square courtyard. "Yet half the women in the solar would give a tooth to have your options right now."

"Stuck within castle walls on a hot day?"

"Betrothed, my dear," she said, "to a young and handsome knight."

The small muscles of her ribs tightened. Last night, Thibaud had brought Aliénor the news of Sir Guy's offer, sharing it as if it were a miracle.

Aliénor said, "We're not betrothed yet."

"But you will be soon."

"It depends on how much Sir Guy will demand for my dowry from the regent."

"The regent is a generous man. The thing is all but done." Blanche leaned in close, hugging Aliénor's arm. "Truly, I don't understand you. He's your countryman, a fine-looking man who is the heir to his father's title—"

"I know, I know. Good sense says I should accept."

"And you *are* a woman of good sense," Blanche added, "yet you're acting as if you'd climb onto the nearest horse and gallop through those gates just to be free of him."

Aliénor flushed, embarrassed she could be read so well. More than once she'd gazed upon the many men-at-arms making the rounds in the field and wondered if she could bribe one to take her away from this place, from this man, from this fate.

But to where?

Aliénor took a sharp turn at the northwest turret

to continue their walk. "Is it so wrong," she said, "to want to love the man I'm to marry?"

"Ah," Blanche said. "So now we come to it. This is about St. Simon, isn't it?"

Even the sound of his name felt like velvet against her ears. "You've been talking to Thibaud."

"Only when forced."

"Yet he confides to you the very secret I've been forbidden to speak."

"Thibaud understands that I have your best interests at heart."

Aliénor sighed, irritation quickly giving way to relief now that she wasn't the only person aware of the weight in her heart.

"Once, long ago," Aliénor said, pushing up her loosely laced sleeves to let the sun kiss her skin, "I'd hoped for no more than kindness and mutual respect from a husband. But since I met Jehan…" *kissed Jehan, made love to Jehan* "…everything has changed."

"True love, then. My dear, this is a rare and wonderful thing, no matter how forbidden or short-lived."

Aliénor sidled a glance to her friend, who looked upon her with a soft smile and a gaze full of understanding.

"Come, do you think you're the only woman who has ever fallen in love?" Blanche squinted past the ramparts as she adjusted her veil. "For me, it was a blacksmith in my father's castle. We had little time together, yet not a day passes without a thought of

Gabriel."

Aliénor covered Blanche's hand with her own. Nearly two decades separated them in age, but for a moment their sentiments resonated as one.

"What you need," Blanche said, "is time. I would suggest waiting several months before the marriage ceremony."

"Months?" She dropped her hand. "As if that would matter."

"You don't want to risk losing the knight's interest, my dear. These days, such offers are few and far between." Blanche pulled her veil down her forehead to better shade her face. "And surely you want your castle back?"

Yes, she wanted her castle, but marrying Guy de Baste would not bring it to her. It would only start a bloody conflict between a husband she'd be stuck with and the man she truly loved.

She loved her castle and she loved Jehan.

She could never have them both.

A shout came from the ramparts, drawing her attention to where a group of knights peered over the battlements.

Blanche's fingers dug into her sleeve. "We should go inside now."

"It's not an attack," she said, as the gears of the portcullis screeched. "The men-at-arms are welcoming someone in."

Horses pounded into the courtyard. The regent led the way, followed by a dozen of his men. The knights in the king's colors were followed by a line of other knights, strangers with pennants of azure and argent, displaying stars and lilies and couchant lions.

No strangers to *her*, she realized with a start. Thibaud's teachings had sunk deep, for she instantly recognized the heraldry of the Count of Foix and the Captal de Buch, riding behind the regent under the white flag of truce.

Blanche sensed her surprise. "You know these men?"

"They're Gascon," she said, "of English loyalties."

Then another knight with English loyalties rode in through the portal. A tall, straight-backed rider with eyes the color of a Gascon sky, whose dark hair tossed in the wind.

CHAPTER TWENTY-THREE

Jehan hovered at the edge of the great hall of the castle at Meaux. He searched the women in the crowd, decked in embroidered silks and jewel-studded girdles, desperate to find the one woman he couldn't get out of his mind.

"I'd have wagered a hundred Parisian pounds that I'd never see you again, St. Simon."

Jehan turned toward the voice and saw Thibaud sauntering toward him, swinging a chalice of wine.

"Good to see you too, Thibaud." He only wished Aliénor trailed in the older man's wake. "You look hale and healthy."

"Tell me about my great-nephew Laurent. Is he safely ensconced in a monastery?"

"Yes."

"Good. At least one of my relatives is safe from you."

Jehan tried to hide his flinch. Thibaud's eyes weren't as friendly as he remembered. Much had changed since the day Laurent had challenged him outside of Castelnau, and none of it for the better.

"Well," Thibaud said, raising his goblet to his lips. "At least you don't deny it."

"Deny what?"

"That it's a suspicious and troubling coincidence to find you here."

"It's no coincidence. The regent insisted we join him for this banquet."

"I'm well aware the Dauphin invited the triumphant warriors to the victory feast. The coincidence is that you should be passing by one particular road to Paris just as the regent and his men were under attack."

"A turn of luck for the regent, wouldn't you say?"

"And how honorable of you to offer your sword in his defense, despite your disparate loyalties."

"There's a truce between the English and French. Hostilities have been put aside. Should I have left your regent to be slaughtered by a mob of peasants armed with pikes?"

"Of course not," Thibaud said. "But I expected you to be in England with the Prince of Wales and your intended wife—rather than suddenly, surprisingly, at my regent's complete disposal."

"I was in London." But not with the intended wife, who was as reluctant as he about the prospect of a marriage. "And now I am not."

"Foix and Buch tell me you're off to a holy war in Prussia."

Jehan frowned, thinking he should have chosen less boastful travelling companions. "I haven't yet committed my sword to the cause."

"A crusade is an honorable diversion during a truce," Thibaud conceded, with a rise of his bushy white brows, "and a fine way to expunge a world of sins."

Jehan's jaw tightened. In truth, the holy war had been nothing but an excuse, the only effective one Jehan could make to secure permission to leave the English court and delay the marriage plans being made for him.

"The curious thing," Thibaud persisted, "is that the route from England to Prussia doesn't ordinarily pass this close to Paris."

"No, it doesn't."

"You've taken a detour, perhaps?"

"I planned to come this way."

Thibaud's expression darkened. "What a foolish waste of time, horse, and money."

"I have to see her, Thibaud."

Truth was a risk, but clearly Thibaud had already guessed it. Jehan figured he wouldn't get any closer to Aliénor without her great-uncle's permission—if not his approval. So Jehan held the older knight's gray gaze, matching Thibaud's growing frustration with a burning determination of his own.

The white-haired knight made a rumbling noise deep in his throat. "You're not doing right by her. She's just beginning to dry her tears."

"She's unhappy?"

"Don't be an idiot."

Jehan looked beyond Thibaud, searching for Aliénor's slim figure among the crowd. Thibaud might be trying to protect his niece, but Jehan was helplessly in love with the woman. Always had been, and likely always would be.

Then his attention fixed on a shining blond head. He shouldered away from the column to sidle one way and then the other, to keep her in view as she wove through the room. His heart beat hard as he glimpsed the rippling wheaten waves of her hair, the curve of her flushed cheek, the glint of firelight off the chain-link belt lying low on her hips. She headed toward the open space where couples gathered for a dance.

Thibaud gripped his arm. "Let her go, Jehan. Seeing you will only cause her pain."

But he'd already yanked away from Thibaud's grip to shoulder through the crowd, ignoring the crush of bodies, the rising chatter, the friendly cheers. He saw nothing else but the slope of her little nose as she stood in profile to him, the slightest of smiles pasted on her face, a frozen smile that held not an ounce of joy.

The music began with a feather of lute strings. A man came around to stand in front of her. Jehan's heart stilled as she dipped in a curtsey before her partner. Watching her dance, Jehan realized he'd forgotten how lithe she was, graceful in her movements. Her hair swung and a flush came to her cheek as she and the man made one full circuit of the ronde.

He couldn't take his eyes off her. Neither could the crowd, it seemed, for a murmuring rose whenever she passed. He was not the only one entranced. He knew it to be true when he glanced, with a jolt of surprise, at her besotted partner.

"You've seen her." Thibaud came up beside him. "Now go."

"She's dancing with Guy de Baste."

"Yes."

What game was de Baste playing? With his own eyes, Jehan had seen this knight slip into the Prince of Wales' tent before the battle at Poitiers. Yet here, only months later, the traitor danced in the castle of the French king, courting Aliénor.

The audacity of the man stunned him.

Then he remembered the nature of this man's relationship to Aliénor and a chill washed over him. "Thibaud—are they married?"

"Not yet."

"Betrothed?"

Thibaud's weary sigh rose above the music, all the confirmation Jehan needed.

Ignoring Thibaud's protests, he strode toward her with a ringing in his head like the clang of church bells. He could only surmise what game Guy de Baste was playing. If de Baste won Aliénor's hand with the French regent's approval, the traitor could then slip off to the Prince of Wales with a claim upon Castelnau the prince was likely to cede—if for no other reason than to pry Jehan away from his "petty Gascon obsessions." Guy would win the castle and the woman as well. After, the traitor could choose whatever loyalty fit best to his own ambitions, without a drop of blood being spilled.

It was a bold, treacherous move. But that wasn't what spread an angry red haze across Jehan's vision as the music stopped and Guy de Baste raised one of Aliénor's hands to his lips.

As if sensing his presence, Aliénor turned his way. His heart leapt as he fell into her soft, brown gaze. He waited for her gasp of surprise, a hand pressed to her chest, some ripple of recognition, but she only curtseyed. She was as pale as the moon, dressed in a fine kirtle and over gown bought with coin from the regent's coffers, no doubt, for he'd never seen such clothing before.

"Sir Jehan," she said. Was it his imagination, or did her voice tremble? "I saw you when you rode into the castle today."

Damn the crowd, he wanted nothing more than to gather her into his arms, but Guy de Baste stepped toward him with a curt nod.

"St. Simon."

Jehan eyeballed the intruder. "De Baste." He

curled his hands into fists. "What a surprise to see you here in the French court."

Not a muscle flickered on the damn knight's face. "I could say the same for you, Sir Jehan."

"I am a guest of your king." His palms itched for the pommel of his sword, not allowed in the dancing-hall, alas. "What king are you a guest of today?"

De Baste was saved by the blast of the dinner trumpet. The traitor took Aliénor's hand and turned a shoulder to Jehan. "Let me escort you, mademoiselle. I know you're very hungry."

Aliénor swept by on a cloud of lavender scent. Jehan stood motionless upon the flagstones as they passed, vaguely aware of the trumpets, of voices raised, of the smell of roasted meat cutting through the ashy scent of burning fires and the choking aroma of frankincense. Only when he felt a tug upon his tunic did he glance at the servant trying to get his attention, a tousled-hair boy wearing the regent's colors, making nervous gestures toward the tables where his Gascon holy warriors were waving him over to the seats of honor.

He walked leadenly to the bench, swung his leg over, and took his place. He stretched his lips at the regent's welcome, bobbed his head in rhythm with his compatriots as the regent stood up to express how grateful he was to have at his table such paragons of chivalry, three knights destined for a holy war yet mindful enough to fight for civility, for justice, for honor and divine right, with hardly a thought to earthly allegiances.

While the regent droned on, Jehan ran his gaze down the length of the opposite table until he found Aliénor seated with her back to him, the sweet curve of her spine as stiff as wood. Guy de Baste, seated across from her, cast glaring looks his way. Did the man have no shame, no honor, no loyalty? De Baste was a traitor playing a dangerous game, marrying above his needs, above his intelligence, above his station, all for damn ambition.

Ambition.

He stared at her until his vision went blurry. Years ago, before he'd sworn allegiance to the prince, he had been a third son with nothing to his name but ambition and a sword. He'd thought it the greatest luck to bend his knee to a rising prince. A prince who cared so little about the castles he conquered that he burned the vexing ones and divvied the rest among his men like biscuits at table, then paraded rewards before hungry knights like trays of roasted swans—all while denying him the one small morsel he craved above all.

When the trumpet blasted for the second course, Jehan jerked to his feet. He took advantage of the distraction to step over the bench, muttering something to his companions about the privy.

He strode through the kitchens to a rear door leading to a garden and a pen full of chickens and goats. Amid the squawking he lifted his head to the sky, streaked with pink. He found the stairs to the ramparts and took them two at a time, nodding brusquely at the men-at-arms who patrolled them. He strode the length until he found a corner atop the southwest tower where he could stare in the direction of Gascony.

He breathed deep, filling his lungs to try to stop the roiling of his mind, the mad turn of his thoughts, the unexpected burn of envy. Guy de Baste shouldn't have her—didn't deserve her—and the damn knight was breaking all the rules to win his prize.

"It's not wise," came a gruff and familiar voice from behind him, "to bolt from a regent's table without word and without cause."

"She's unhappy, Thibaud."

"Her happiness is no longer your concern."

"Her happiness will *always* be my concern."

"Then don't interfere in this betrothal."

"Guy de Baste is no prize. His loyalties are suspect. I can prove it."

"Because you saw him at the English court? Or with the Prince of Wales?"

Jehan pivoted to face the older knight.

"Guy de Baste is a spy for the French," Thibaud said. "He's been working for the crown for a very long time."

Jehan glared at Thibaud and his wild wooly hair tinged pink by the sunset, dumbfounded by this revelation, waiting for the envy and wrath burning in his gut to ebb. But the fact that Guy de Baste wasn't a traitor to his king—that there was no intrigue afoot—

that de Baste might be a more loyal man than Jehan had ever expected—none of that changed anything. Jehan still roiled with anger and jealousy, teetering on madness at the thought of *any* man, no matter how worthy, stepping between him and the woman he loved.

But now there was something else pricking at his conscience. Thibaud's revelation had torn a veil from his eyes. It came to him, in a blinding rush, exactly what had been bothering him most about Guy de Baste.

What kind of man dares to break solemn vows, to discard all fealties to princes and kings, and casts all danger to the winds to get the one single thing he wants above all others?

De Baste, so he'd thought.

So Jehan had despised the knight.

But perhaps it was really *envy*.

"Thibaud," he barked, as breath rushed into his lungs, "you must be close to the throne if the regent confides such secrets to you."

Thibaud made a scoffing noise. "I have the regent's ear, his trust, and his absolute confidence as I had with his grandfather before him—"

"Then get me an audience with him."

"Why?" The older knight hiked his fists on his hips. "So you can break her heart again?"

"No," he said, grinning as he slapped his hands on Thibaud's shoulders. "So I can make it whole."

CHAPTER TWENTY-FOUR

"Aliénor." Blanche hiked her hands upon her hips. "Didn't you hear the summons? The regent has called everyone to the great hall."

"You go on ahead." Aliénor didn't raise her head from her embroidery though the room had come alive with the rustling of skirts. "I have to a rose to finish."

"A sad-looking one, too. In any case, the embroidery can wait. The assembly won't."

"I don't need to hear any more bad news about riots in Paris, Blanche."

"This melancholy doesn't suit you."

She dipped her head. Guy de Baste had said much the same thing at table the night before, his smile going thin as she answered all his questions in single sentences, and never ventured any queries of her own.

Blanche said, "He might be there, you know."

Blanche didn't have to say the name for Aliénor to know of whom she spoke. No man filled her mind like Jehan. How wild he'd looked when he'd approached her last night. His dark hair fell long below his shoulders. There were shadows around his eyes and inside them, too. How she had ached to run her fingers through the stubble of his three-day beard, drawn by the current vibrating between them.

"Aliénor," Blanche began on a sigh.

"I'm sure he's gone," she said. Jehan had disappeared long before dinner ended last night. And through the open windows of the solar, she had heard horses coming and going all morning. "It's a long way to Prussia."

"Or he could be waiting downstairs to say farewell to the prince."

She flinched as her needle slipped and found its way into flesh. She sucked her thumb into her mouth, numbing the pain. She only wished she could numb all pain so easily, including how much it hurt to love.

But Blanche was standing in front of her, hands on ample hips, unrelenting.

With a sigh, she put aside her embroidery.

In the main hall, excitement vibrated to the rafters. People chattered and jostled for position. Blanche used her bulk as well as her prerogative to find a place close to the action, where Aliénor intended to lean against a pillar and think of nothing.

But when Aliénor saw who waited in the empty space in front of the regent's table, her shield of numbness shattered.

Jehan was dressed in black hose, a scarlet tunic, and a shirt as bright as a fuller could make it. She'd seen such clothing once before, when her brother Bertrand had bent a knee in church to be dubbed a knight. The scarlet tunic stood for the blood Bertrand might shed for God, king, and honor; the black of his hose stood for the death that must be faced without fear; and the white of the shirt represented purity of soul and character.

"Sir Jehan," the regent said, lifting a parchment from his table. "I understand you are in possession of a castle in the Gascon borderlands, once owned by my late knight the Viscount de Tournan."

Were it not for the column of stone at her shoulder, she would slide into a heap upon the floor.

"Yes," Jehan said. "Castelnau-sur-Arrats."

"Seized by you?"

"Yes."

"By force of arms?"

"In a time of war."

"By order of the Prince of Wales."

"And with his help," he added, "for it's a strong castle, well-managed by the family, positioned on a promontory overlooking a sweep of fertile land."

"Has the English prince gifted this stolen castle into your care as a reward for your loyalty?"

"It is in my physical possession, but the prince

has made only promises."

"The English prince," the regent repeated, "your liege lord."

"Yes, Your Grace."

"And yet today, you stand before me, offering to cede the castle back to France."

Aliénor pressed a hand against her heart. The skin vibrated against her palm. Why would Jehan surrender the castle? Had the prince found him a rich wife?

"I cede it to you," Jehan said, "and your father the king, upon my own free will. And with it, I offer to pay homage."

A shivering whisper of surprise shuddered through the hall as her thoughts raced in a thousand directions.

The regent said, "Does your liege lord, the Prince of Wales, know what you are offering me?"

"He does not."

"You defy him."

"I do, Your Grace."

"And how am I to trust a man who breaks a solemn vow?"

"Because I break this vow in order to right a wrong. There is one, single condition to my offer."

Aliénor's fingertips started to tingle and she realized Blanche was gripping her hand like a vice.

"This condition," the regent said, "no doubt involves the heiress to the castle, the lovely sister of the brave, crippled Gascon boy Thibaud has told me so much about."

The regent had not spoken her name, but heads turned nonetheless, skirts rustled, sword sheathes jangled, and she felt the heat of the perusal of those around her like the blaze of torchlight upon her face.

"Everything I do today is for the lady." Jehan lowered himself to one knee and held out his sword, flat between his outstretched hands. "Your Grace, I offer you the castle, my loyalty, and my sword—everything I possess—in return for my heart's one and only desire: Aliénor de Tournan, as my wife."

***

As Jehan's proclamation echoed in the rafters, Aliénor stepped back, and then stepped back again. She ignored the whispers and stares as she pivoted on one foot and headed toward the front door of the great hall. She wasn't sure what propelled her away from the ceremony—shock or instinct or just the need to *breathe*—but she didn't stop in the courtyard. She passed kitchen maids chatting as they pulled water from the well, stable boys dozing, and men heaping hay into troughs for the horses, increasing her pace to a run as she headed toward the castle portal.

Outside the cool tunnel, the sun warmed her hair, braised her cheeks, and stoked her thrumming excitement. The air smelled of warm grass and recent rain, and she knew she was standing on it only when she felt moisture soaking through her slippers.

She turned her face to the sky. Had she imagined what she'd just seen? Was she dreaming? Certainly she must have misunderstood what was said. Or had Jehan really just offered himself up as a knight to the king of France?

A clatter of hooves upon paving stones made her swirl around, but the rider leaving the castle was not Jehan. At the sight of her, the knight stopped, his mount kicking up gravel so fiercely that a shower of stones sprayed her leather-clad feet.

Guy de Baste said, "I see by your expression, my lady, that this news was as much a surprise to you as it was to me."

Words were impossible, she could barely think.

"It's a pity our plans have gone awry." Guy de Baste's reluctant smile held no humor. "But I suspect you won't mourn me, eh?"

Indeed, she would not. The force and clarity of that singular thought knocked the fog from her senses. She had been numb since Sir Guy had made his offer, but as the numbness dissipated she realized she would never have vowed before God to be this man's wife. She was no longer the girl she'd been before Jehan stormed into her life. She would never again consider offering her hand without offering her heart, as well.

Even a convent would have been better than a loveless marriage.

"The regent is generous," she said. "Perhaps he'll

suggest another dispossessed heiress, or a rich widow."

"Rich widow or not, sweet Aliénor, none will be as lovely as you."

Gallant to the last. She granted him a smile. "I wish you great fortune, Sir Guy."

"And to you. *Adieu, ma chou.*"

Sir Guy kicked his horse and headed along the path toward where the gate opened to the bridge across the river.

But she didn't follow the path of his passing, for when Sir Guy moved away from the portal, another silhouette stepped out of the shadows.

CHAPTER TWENTY-FIVE

How young he looked, dressed in his scarlet and white like a knight fresh to the sword. A light wind ruffled his hair and brought back a thousand memories of him standing upon the ramparts of Castelnau. Aliénor knew she shouldn't be able to see his blue eyes so clearly from where she stood in the bright of the sun, but she could indeed see his gaze. By the look on his face, he was as buffeted as she was by the same powerful emotions.

He crossed the graveled path, moving with patience, as if he were afraid he'd frighten her away. Watching his legs flex and his shoulders slope and his dark, dear head sway as he ventured ever closer riffled her senses in ways she'd forbidden herself to imagine during the long, lonely months of their separation. Now she embraced the flood of those feelings, letting herself experience everything once too painful to relive.

He stopped a few steps away from her and

glanced over her shoulder toward the far gate. "Did he make you another offer?"

"Sir Guy?"

"He chased you when you left the hall."

She shook her head. "He just paused long enough to say good-bye."

"Good." One of the lines on his brow smoothed. "Because if he had swept you onto his horse and whisked you away—"

"I would have been just as surprised as you."

A smile slipped across his lips. "He's a fool for letting you go so easily, Aliénor."

She gripped a tippet in her hands for balance, for if Jehan kept looking at her like this, she would never be able to maintain composure.

"You know," she said, riffling her fingers through the pelt of fur, "you might have given me fair warning about all this."

"I wanted to." He shifted his weight, daring to come a step closer. "Thibaud forbade me to say anything. He insisted we hear the regent's decision first."

Stubborn Thibaud. Yet she couldn't be angry at her great-uncle, knowing he was trying to protect her, as always.

"When I went to London," he said, "I tried to convince the prince to let me marry you, *couret*. But he refused to consider it, even to listen."

"Indeed, he would have no reason to allow it."

"That's true, if a man's only aim in life is

ambition." A muscle in his cheek flexed and his hands did, too, and a look akin to guilt flittered across his face. "After this last campaign, I saw my prince with a clearer eye. He's a man who stands second in line to the throne, who has the whole Christian world laid out before him, who has never really known hunger or cold or despair. And yet in a time of peace, he does nothing more than prepare for the next war so he may gain more castles, more lands, more power—and dangle them before us, before *me,* without considering what I, or any of his knights, or the whole of England, truly desires in our heart of hearts."

She looked up past the wool of the scarlet tunic stretched across his shoulders, to the tightness of his jaw, aching to ease his guilt.

"So," she murmured, "no English widow after all?"

He rolled one of those massive shoulders. "I'm doing both the widow and myself a great favor."

"Was she not rich enough?"

"She had three castles," he said, "as well as the title of marchioness."

"Was she not young enough?"

He made a grunting noise. "Time yet for childbearing."

She raised a brow. "Not pretty enough, then?"

"The real problem, Aliénor, was that she wasn't *you.*"

Then he lowered his mighty body, those broad and endless shoulders, that rock-hard stretch of chest.

That all passed before her eyes as he sank to one knee, just as he'd done in the great hall before the regent.

He whispered, "Do you despise me, *couret?*"

She shook her head, confused.

"For shifting loyalties," he said, his expression serious. "For abandoning my oath of fealty to the English in favor of the French."

"How could I despise you?" The sweet aroma of the sacred oil wafted toward her from where the bishop must have touched his brow. "You did it all for me."

"I did it for the woman I love."

She heard horses' hooves clanking on the cobblestones outside the castle wall, carts creaking and swaying, peddlers calling their wares, wind riffling along the grass, birds twittering as they set upon the grain that had fallen off a wagon. She heard women laughing by the well, men boasting upon the ramparts, a pig squealing in a pen behind the donjon, and above all, her pulse pounding like a minstrel's drum in her ears.

"Aliénor," he said, uncertainty on his face. "I have nothing to offer you but that which you already consider your own."

Something wet rolled down her face, despite the lack of rain. "You can give me your heart, Jehan."

"It has always been yours." He took her hand and flattened her palm on his chest. "From the beginning and now—if you'll take me as your lawful husband—until the end."

A husky sound left her throat, a half-laugh. The grass felt soft beneath her knees as she knelt before him. How sturdy his shoulders under her hands.

"Marry me," he whispered. "Marry me and be my wife."

"Yes."

He captured her answer with his mouth. For long and breathless moments, she curled into his warmth, pressed against his familiar chest, and breathed in the scent of his skin while their kiss deepened.

When he finally pulled away, a smile broke over his face like sunshine coming from behind a cloud.

"Make me one more promise, Jehan."

"Anything."

"Once we're wed," she said, "take me home."

***

Home.

Aliénor had not expected to feel like this, but the minute they rode over the last hill and she saw the rolling vineyards and watched the sunlight gleam upon the limestone walls of Castelnau-sur-Arrats, her heart swelled to the point where it hardly left her room to breathe.

"Was there ever such a sight, Jehan?"

"Never," he said, with a knowing laugh. "It's the finest castle in all of Gascony." He cast her a sidelong glance. "Although considering how often we've camped upon rocky ground these past weeks, I'd be transported by the sight of any place that promised a proper bed within."

She smiled his way as the memory of the journey passed between them. Though they'd spent their wedding night proper in a fine room in the castle at Meaux, they took to the road the very next day. Since then, they'd made do under a linen tent, creating warmth where there was no fire. When necessary, they'd snuck away to quiet coves and the cover of the woods to indulge their urges.

A warmth rose at the memory of last night's loving in particular. His kisses on her thighs, the intensity of the sensation, her fingers lost in his long, soft hair…

"Woman," he growled, "if you keep looking at me like that…"

"Like what?"

"Up from under your lashes with mischief in your eyes."

Her womb tightened as his gaze intensified. Her back might still be bruised from the hard ground—and his, too, she thought with a flush—but her body still throbbed, hungry at the pleasures to come.

"No more, *couret*. There's a mile between here and the bed, and you're making it uncomfortable for me to sit this horse."

"Then what are we waiting for?" She leaned over her horse to kick it into a gallop.

He reached over to seize the reins. "We talked

about this."

"Jehan, don't coddle me."

"I'll coddle you all I like." His smile was wicked.

"You don't know if—"

"Six weeks, *couret.*"

"That isn't unusual at all."

"I can feel the changes," he said, "in the softness of your breasts, the fullness of your body under my palms, the way you wake and eat like a starving woman—"

"I'm a happily married woman, of course I eat heartily." She retrieved her reins and veered away from him, giving him an eye. "But if you want to check my breasts again, you won't hear me complaining."

She kicked her horse and surged ahead. With a grunt he caught up and surpassed her, riding in front to set a brisk, but not reckless, pace. With a lightness of heart, she nudged her mare in pursuit, fixing her gaze on Jehan's fine broad back, the stream of his dark hair, and the tightness of his thighs as he rode. They raced down the gentle slope and through the paths of the vineyard, kicking up dirt as they went.

The horses, though wearied, must have sensed the end of the journey for they headed straight toward the bridge. Once on the other side, they were forced to slow and pause, for the villagers surged from their homes to surround them. She was gratified to see how healthy and well-fed everyone looked. She reached down to accept a bouquet of wildflowers from one of the children while Jehan pulled out his satchel and showered the crowd with coins.

Three men awaited them at the base of the slope. Two men-at-arms, and in the middle—

"Laurent!"

Her brother kicked his mount to meet her. He'd grown a full, dark beard that made him look as swarthy and dangerous as a highwayman.

His black eyes locked on hers. "Is it true then? You are married?"

"Well good day to you, too," she teased. "How did you find out?"

"Thibaud sent a message to the monastery in Toulouse. You must have taken the long route home for me to beat you here." Laurent dipped his head as Jehan rode to her side. "I broke my promise not to leave the confines of the monastery, Sir Jehan. I ask your forgiveness."

"Some promises," Jehan said, "are worth breaking."

Laurent's face brightened. "Tell me my sister isn't pulling wool over my head. You've truly wed?"

"We are now brothers-in-law," Jehan said drily.

"I trust you will treat her well?"

"I have vowed so, until death do us part."

Laurent eyed Jehan in an odd, intense way that made Aliénor wonder what they were teaching him in the monastery. But then, surprisingly, Jehan kicked his horse closer and Laurent and Jehan's arms clashed in a clatter of chain mail and flesh and leather and bone. She watched as they gripped one another by the forearm and moved as if they were trying to wrestle each other off their horses, laughing all the while.

Men, she thought. She would never understand them.

When the wrestling match was over, Laurent kicked his horse to her side. She leaned over to embrace him, unbalanced, their legs crushed between their horses.

"You look well, Ally," he said.

"You look hairy."

He rubbed his beard in a bashful way and she saw, finally, a glimpse of the boy under the countenance of the man. "The monastery cells are cold."

"So now you believe me?"

"Alas."

"I missed you at the wedding, you know."

"I suppose Thibaud had the honor of giving you away."

"Indeed he did."

"At least I didn't have to beat him in a sword fight to win the right." Laurent glanced behind them, seeking something or someone. "Our great-uncle didn't return with you?"

"He has a reason to stay in Paris." She grinned, thinking of how she'd come upon Thibaud and Blanche embracing in an alcove during her wedding feast. "He belongs in the king's court, Laurent, like a duck belongs in water. With a kinder man ruling

Castelnau, Thibaud feels he can indulge his own preferences."

Laurent nodded. "It must have been a fine wedding."

"It would have been even lovelier had you presided over the vows."

"I'm not anointed," he said, his gaze skittering away. "I may never be."

She jolted on her saddle. "Laurent?"

"Ally, did you not once say to me that every man—or woman—should be free to choose his own destiny?"

"Yes, but—"

"This castle is yours. Don't worry on that account. You have always deserved it and I make no claim."

"But—"

"Ally," he interrupted again, raising one hand. "The world is bigger and more complicated than I ever imagined. For now, can we leave it at that?"

"For now," she said, her head swimming. "But we will talk later, *frai,* and there'll be no wiggling out of it."

Soon they rose over the crest to the open field and then, by silent consent, they all cantered for the drawbridge. Once through the open portcullis, they pulled their mounts to a stop. Jehan's men-at-arms as well as her father's former vassals all gathered to welcome them, dressed in their best. She took Sir Rostand's hand to dismount and greeted a teary

Margot and a shuffling, bashful Hugo and a flushed Sir Rudel. Then, realizing without a proper chatelaine, there was no one to give orders for food and drink, she abandoned Jehan and Laurent to deal with the horses so she could play the chatelaine once again.

It was well beyond dark when she finally left the main hall to climb to the tower room where she and Jehan had spent so many wonderful evenings last winter. She entered to find her husband reclining in their bed, awash in the glow of the fire, as naked as the day he was born.

He said, "I've been waiting for you."

"I see," she grinned, reaching back to loosen the ties of her kirtle. "I didn't even see you slip away from the great hall."

"You were distracted by something in the kitchens."

"I'm not distracted anymore."

She walked into the light, enjoying the way his gaze roamed over her body. She hiked her skirts and climbed shamelessly upon his lap. He wound an arm around her, drawing her close enough to feel exactly how excited he was. When her loosened kirtle slipped off her shoulder, he nuzzled her throat, giving her little love bites that made her toes curl.

She closed her eyes and reveled in his touch. She didn't care that she'd not yet spoken about the plans for tomorrow, or asked how much wine had come in during the last season, or checked the stores. She didn't care that the dust of travel still stained her kirtle and the bristles on his unshaven cheek scraped her skin. All she cared about was the sharp, longed-for pressure of his lips and the warmth of his body against hers.

But there was one tiny little thing still troubling her, something not so easy to ignore. When he paused from running kisses down her neck to fuss with the laces of her neckline, she seized the moment.

"I have an idea, Jehan," she whispered.

"So do I—"

"No, I mean, about Castétis."

"Castétis," he muttered, breathing hard as he picked at a stubborn knot. "Why are we talking about Castétis?"

"It needs a lord of its own," she said. "Don't you think?"

He glanced up at her, raising a brow. "The only lord I want you thinking about right now is the one–"

"I'm thinking about Laurent." She grasped his hands to get his attention. "He's reconsidering his vocation."

He blinked at her for a long, blank moment.

"I thought, maybe," she ventured, "he could manage Castétis."

He breathed a husky laugh. "Still negotiating ransom, are we?"

"Well." She lifted one of his hands to her mouth and kissed his knuckles. "I'm not suggesting you *give* it to him." Not yet, anyway, not until Laury had figured out what he truly wanted in life. "I'm suggesting he act as steward or—"

"Consider it done."

"Jehan?"

"Castétis is yours," he said. "It was yours the moment you said 'I do'."

She looked at him softly, thinking about ambition and love and how much this knight had given up, all for her.

"Are we done with requests now, woman?" He asked with a twinkle in his eye. "Because I've got other plans for the evening."

"One more thing."

He groaned, pulling his hands from hers and then gripping her hips. "Tell the chatelaine to go away," he said, "and bring me back my wife."

"Make me a promise."

"You're killing me, *couret*."

"I want to bring life back into this castle." She couldn't wait to restore her home to how it had once been—full of laughter and shouts and music and *people*. "This child will be in the cradle by next summer, but I want another firm in my belly before Christmas next. Can you promise me that?"

His lips spread in a lazy smile as he shifted her into a position that made her whole body tremble.

"As you wish, my love," he said. "Our new life begins tonight."

*****

ABOUT THE AUTHOR

Lisa Ann Verge is the critically acclaimed RITA© nominated author of eighteen novels that have been published worldwide and translated into as many languages.

She started her career writing emotionally intense romance about hot men and dangerous women, and now as **Lisa Verge Higgins** she also writes life-affirming women's fiction.

A finalist for RT Book Review awards five times over, Lisa has won the Golden Leaf and the Bean Pot, and twice she has cracked Barnes & Noble's General Fiction Forum's top twenty books of the year. She currently lives in New Jersey with her husband and their three daughters, who never fail to make life interesting.